Praise for *Her*

Her Golden Coast is a razor-sharp insight into San Francisco's tech scene. With astute observations on gender, class and privilege, it perfectly captures – and skewers – one of the world's richest cities and the unique blend of people that occupy it. Behind the bite and wit, however, is a tenderly rendered queer love story that gives the novel a warm and beating heart. I'll be thinking about Laurie and Mal for a long time to come.

> — **Kia Abdullah**, Author of Times Bestseller
> THOSE PEOPLE NEXT DOOR

From the first page, Deracine's vivid descriptions and masterful storytelling draw you into the vibrant yet tumultuous world of Silicon Valley. The authenticity with which the author portrays the tech scene and the world of publishing—the ambition, cutthroat competition, and hypocrisy—is both eye-opening and captivating. What truly sets this novel apart is its fearless exploration of queer love in a modern context while grappling with themes of individual purpose, societal definitions of success and status, and the value of art (and artists). Deracine handles these themes with grace and sensitivity, providing a refreshing perspective that is both heartfelt and empowering. The romance is genuine and profound, making you root for the protagonists, Mal(ini) and Laurie, every step of the way.

> — **Osman Haneef**, Author of THE VERDICT
> and winner of the UBL literary award

Her Golden Coast offers a queer female consciousness to the Kerouac tradition of self-discovery at a breathless pace. It targets an audience of women (X-ennials and earlier) who came of age when sexuality and socioeconomic status had no real fluidity, and builds a place of hard-won permission for those who also struggle with or strangle within a capitalistic patriarchy despite the clear signs of its failing and dissolution.

— **Caroline Manring,** Author of *MANUAL FOR EXTINCTION* and *CERULEANA,* winner of the National Poetry Review Book Prize

> Dear Irene,
> Thank you for coming out to support me & this book!
> ♡ Anat Deracine

her golden coast

anat deracine

Copyright © 2024 Anat Deracine.

All rights reserved.

This novel is entirely a work of fiction. The names, characters and incidents portrayed in it are the work of the author's imagination. Any resemblance to actual persons, living or dead, is entirely coincidental.

No part of this publication may be reproduced, stored in a retrieval system, used or transmitted, in any form or by any means, without the express written permission of the publisher except for the use of brief quotations in a book review.

Mayavin Publishing

ISBN ebook: 979-8-9908352-1-4
ISBN paperback: 979-8-9908352-0-7

anatderacine.com

for every woman who ever thought

she was in it alone

and who is still learning

to ask for help

chapter one

a gorgeous, grapy dusk fell over the Bay Bridge, but the hills beyond were the color of ash and wildfires. Laurie stared at it over her computer screen, aching sometimes to paint the wine-splashed sky and sometimes at the thought of the burning vineyards.

"Beautiful, isn't it?" Vic said, stalking over to the window to obstruct her view. Her boss stretched his arms above his head so his shirt rode up, exposing the crack of his ass. When Laurie said nothing, he turned to face her. "Got plans for the weekend?"

"Cam's picking me up in a bit," she said.

"Ah, still going strong then? It's been a while, no?"

"A year."

Vic nodded. The glint in his eyes was familiar. She'd seen it on circling turkey vultures. In California, a year was a lifetime. Long enough for startups to fly or die, and long enough to be the point in the relationship when every question was a final exam in disguise.

Cam arrived. The men tilted their heads up towards each other, a reverse-nod of acknowledgement at her seamless transfer from employer to boyfriend.

She grabbed her things and slipped her hand into Cam's, tugging lightly to indicate her hurry. They said their goodbyes and headed towards the BART.

"My place?" she asked, when they got on the train headed to the Mission district. "I need to veg out. We can order in."

A small frown appeared on Cam's face. "But we're meeting Will for dinner tonight, aren't we?"

Oh. Was it that time of the month already? She bit her lip, thinking of how she could beg off or ask for a raincheck.

And still pass the final exam.

"It's not about us," Cam said, nuzzling her neck. "Will's got no one else."

Laurie's shoulders sagged. She should have guessed. *Will*. Every time she thought Cam might take the next step and ask her to move in, Will dragged her boyfriend back to their raucous college life like some vestigial Sherlock for one last case. Cam was always apologetic afterwards, full of compliments about how she 'brought out the best in him' that her mother told her were the mark of a keeper, but Laurie always thought they made her out to be broccoli—fibrous but unappealing.

Particularly tonight, when Cam's glowing skin and hair only served as a reminder of her own premenstrual frizz and bloat. Still, *not about us* meant that there was an *us* in play—the kind of *us* that shared views on healthcare policy and took care of lonely friends.

Just before they stepped out of the train, Cam adjusted his curls by the reflection in the BART window. He kept an eye open for taxis. She didn't bother, but he was an idealist. Most techies were. They couldn't load a dishwasher but somehow believed they could end war and world hunger. Of course he thought he could find a taxi on a Friday night. She and Cam were equidistant from twenty-five on either side, but sometimes she felt the gap widening. It wasn't his fault. In California, there were no seasons. Years were counted in video game releases.

They walked past the Mission's loud churches and louder mortuaries, past elegant pastel houses punctuated by alleys with swirling technicolor graffiti. Laurie shrank slightly at the enormous, brown-skinned naked women that glared at her from these walls. Women certain of their meaning: *you don't even dare paint us, never mind be us.*

She looked away, catching sight of a skinny man with a light, scruffy beard. His salmon pink T-shirt said *Men for breast cancer*, the critical word (*awareness*) hidden beneath the zipper of a black hoodie. She smiled. She would've nudged Cam, but he was walking faster than usual.

Tonight's taqueria had the technicolor tiles of a CW drama. Laurie's stomach growled, and Cam asked for chips and salsa. His attentiveness buoyed her mood a little.

"I don't understand why Will's always so late," Cam said. "Don't you work together? He could have just joined us."

Laurie's shoulders tightened. She and Will might work at the same tech Unicorn, but he wasn't her responsibility. He was a software engineer, strolling into work at ten-thirty with the swagger of someone who didn't need this job too badly. She was an admin to his boss. Vic had hired her out of a bar for her ability to hold billionaires' heads over the toilet and keep her mouth shut about it. She worked sixty-hour weeks, but her salary was a third of Will's and she had no equity. She shared office space with techies, but little else.

Once, a visitor blurted out the question—what brought you to tech?—and Vic had guffawed as he said, "She peoples well."

She'd said nothing. Vic had brought her into the Unicorn

in the same way he picked up intriguing statues in Japan and Bhutan on his vacations. Statues didn't speak, and part of *peopling* well was letting bosses think they were funny.

"There he is," she said, seeing Will.

Cam looked over, and his face crumpled so suddenly that an incredulous laugh escaped Laurie's lips before she could stop it. It was the betrayed look on Cam's face that set it off. Will hadn't been silent about it when Cam switched out game night for date night, and now he'd brought a date himself?

Will's jeans were rolled up over his right ankle, the stretch of skin there marked with grease from the bicycle chain. His large hands slid low over a woman's backside, fingers stretched out trying to encompass her. His eyes moved from her to the selection of burrito fillings, as if uncertain where to begin.

Laurie had heard a rumor there was a spreadsheet where Will's coworkers tracked his girlfriends, with photographs, dates and timestamps (a few years later, they'd spend this same energy hunting Pokemon). She'd never cared before, but for some reason the thought of this woman going into that sheet twinged through her belly with an unpleasant cramp.

"Will!"

At Cam's call, Will bit the woman's ear and whispered something into it. A slow smile spread over her face and she kissed him. It was the kind of kiss no makeup could survive, one that made it as uncomfortable to watch as it was impossible to look away.

The woman wasn't conventionally beautiful, but there was something striking about her that meant that when she and Will walked over, Laurie got up instinctively, then stood swaying in confusion. She hadn't meant to offer up her own chair. Meanwhile the waiter, who had ignored them for five minutes when she wanted chips, quickly brought over another chair.

The woman—Mal—thanked him with a casual wave that suggested she was used to this, that people often fell over themselves trying to please her, and it was only right that they did. The waiter stood taller, smiling broadly, as if he'd only been waiting for her to pluck him out of obscurity and realize his potential. His simpering obedience made Laurie cringe—hopefully she hadn't come across as desperate for Mal's approval when she'd offered her chair.

Everywhere she went in San Francisco, she was haunted by the specter of the people she might have been if not for Vic, might yet become one day. A slightly stoned barista here. A frazzled waitress there. Just last night, a stern Walgreens clerk who sneered at her purchase of condoms.

She shifted closer to Cam to make room, and also to put some distance between them and the other couple. Especially Will. Cam had got her used to thinking all men smelled of L'Occitane aftershave, so Will was always a rude shock. He radiated heat, and the air around him was thick with exertion and bicycle grease.

Not just him, Laurie realized, wrinkling her nose.

Mal crossed one leg high over the other, like a man, as she sat down. Beyond the edge of the table, her foot swirled lazily in its boot. They'd biked here together. Somehow that stuck in Laurie's craw more than anything else. Men had already stopped paying for dates. The least they could do was pick a girl up.

Mal fixed her with a look. "We've met before?"

It wasn't really a question, not the way she said it. Cam looked at Laurie expectantly. As if her admin duties had extended beyond working hours and it was her fault this dinner wasn't what Cam wanted it to be.

It was Will who finally said, "You must've seen Laurie at the office. She works for Vic."

Mal's face brightened. "I thought I'd be the only woman on the team. I'm transferring over to Vic on Monday."

"Won't that be awkward?" Cam said, brows furrowed as he looked between Mal and Will. "Being involved with someone on your team?"

"Not for long," Will said, reaching for the chips. "I'm quitting."

Cam's hand stopped in mid-air, the chip in his fingers fluttering, fragile as a butterfly. "What do you—?"

But the waiter was here again. Will and Cam ordered flautas and a pitcher of margarita. Laurie got the chili con queso, and Cam turned to her surprised—he was severely allergic to dairy and capsaicin.

She hid the guilty flinch and the burn of resentment in the bite of a taco. If Cam and Will were going to get drunk on margaritas, what did it matter what she did? These nights only ever ended one way. She lived in the Mission, close to more taquerias and bars than they'd been able to hit in a year, so *Let's have dinner with Will* meant she'd go home alone stewing, not having said *I didn't have any booze, so maybe let's not split the bill*, and Cam would stagger in at 2 AM, singing tunelessly and stinking of tequila and rum, nuzzling up to her until she forgave him.

"Got to cut the umbilical sometime," Will said, making a slicing motion, "before the corporation suffocates your soul."

"What will you do instead?" Laurie asked, surprised at the twinge of regret.

"I'll be spending the winter in Tahoe. Skiing, maybe becoming a ski instructor. I'll think about what I want to do after the snow melts. I've always wanted to hike the Appalachian Trail."

Her nostrils flared with the effort not to smile. No more dinners!

Cam looked as if he'd eaten an entire jalapeño. "That doesn't seem very strategic. What if the IPO happens while you're gone?"

Strategic. It was a word that came up every day at the Unicorn. It was *supposed* to mean the ability to think ahead. The way techies used it, it meant *I want to say you're being childish, but then HR will yell at me, so I'm just going to say you're not being strategic.*

Will phoning in rich before his thirtieth birthday citing a case of the *don't-wannas* probably wasn't strategic. But at least it meant he and Cam wouldn't go off for that planned camping trip to Death Valley next month either. Good. Adding existential dread and sunburn to a Thanksgiving vacation didn't seem strategic either.

Mal was looking at her, dark eyes taking in her expression while yielding nothing of her own thoughts. Laurie struggled to look away when their eyes caught, as if an invisible web drew them together.

"Climbing the corporate ladder gives the illusion of progress," Will said. "It's time to let go of structure, leave Diaspar. Too many people hold on to what's in front of them, even when it makes them miserable."

He hadn't directed any of this at Laurie, but she winced. Then she noticed Mal's eyes on her again.

"And you—" Cam said, turning to Mal, "you aren't going to convince him to stay?"

"Far from it," Mal said, leaning back in her chair as if this was nothing to her. "There's a crash coming, and valuations are going to fall. There's no way we'll IPO for the next two years. I'm just willing to wait it out."

Laurie pretended to be engrossed in her food. Every time someone said IPO she remembered how she and Cam had their first real date at a bar serving IPO Pale Ale. For months afterwards, she'd believed an IPO was a kind of beer. Cam always looked at her fondly when someone talked stocks. Her ears warmed under his gaze now.

"IPOs are a value trap," Will said.

"A value trap?" Cam asked.

"It's when you're unwilling to renegotiate your current situation because you're committed to past values," Laurie said, recognizing Will's reference to *Zen and the Art of Motorcycle Maintenance*. Another part of *peopling* well was learning what made her coworkers tick, and there wasn't a week that went by that Will didn't reference the Beats.

Strange that Cam hadn't picked up on it first. When they'd first started going out, she hadn't been able to pick up his references. It felt like a class marker, whether someone spoke in book quotes or movie quotes—although Cam didn't believe in class. He didn't know how voraciously she read, how she still felt she was running to catch up.

"Ah, sunk cost," Mal said, with an admiring nod that made Laurie puff up almost as much as the waiter had. "Although, in San Francisco, everyone's constantly renegotiating everything. New jobs, new relationships, new therapists. It's a bit exhausting, to be so constantly on the cusp of change. Just find yourself already. Commit to something. Anything. So, sure, hike across America. Wear comfortable shoes."

"Finding yourself is getting more and more expensive," Will said. "The trail's going to set me back at least six grand."

Laurie nearly gagged. After rent, she had five hundred dollars in the bank. Why should it cost twelve times that to walk around a free country?

"Remember El Paso?" Cam said suddenly. "We managed that hike on ten bucks a day." He laughed. "We were high all the time on mescaline and Carlos Castaneda, looking for conviction beyond the Lutheran church."

To her surprise, Will didn't add in his own story as he usually did, raving about some girl or drug. She hadn't thought him capable of either self-awareness or restraint. Now, knowing he'd be gone soon, she was seeing his more attractive features. His unrepentant lust for life that kept Cam in his orbit. His curiosity, which led him as often to books as it did to pharmaceuticals.

Half the things Cam had introduced her to—biking the Golden Gate, hiking Mount Tam, eating sushi—he'd done with Will first. It used to make her jealous; tonight, it suddenly left her unsettled. Without Will, who would Cam be?

"How long have you two known each other?" Mal asked, gesturing between the two men as if the same question was on her mind.

"Since college," Cam said. "He knocked on my door with a colander on his head, promising me a party where there would be three score queens, and four score concubines and virgins without number."

"The Song of Solomon," Laurie said, and then felt guilty when Will's eyes turned to her in pleasant surprise. Annoyance followed so quickly she wondered if the chili con queso was to blame for the sudden mood-swings. She wasn't betraying Cam;

it wasn't her fault Will could ignite a spark with Tupperware.

"Cam was a bit stodgy in college," Will said, his powerful, muscled frame making Cam seem smaller even though he was six feet tall. "Wouldn't drink because it was against the law. Hadn't even popped his cherry yet."

"Is that so?" Mal asked. But there was something sharp in her tone, a strange wariness.

"I'll be back," Laurie said, getting up to go to the bathroom. Instinct told her an explosion seemed imminent, and she didn't want to be caught in the middle.

"I'll come with," Mal said. "Leave you two some time to catch up." She stuck her hands into her pockets and followed Laurie into the small bathroom, sat on the sink while she went into the stall.

Why couldn't she just wait outside?

"Can I ask you something?" Mal asked, making conversation as if completely unbothered by the sound of trickling from the stall. "Do you know if Cam and Will have ever slept together?"

Laurie rushed to flush so she could get out and see her face, decide if this woman was for real. She'd meant to come off outraged, but dropped her purse and came out of the stall stumbling, snatching at a lipstick and a mostly-gone roll of mints as they rolled in separate directions on the tiles.

"Well, they're a little bit in love with each other, aren't they?"

She was about to protest, and then suddenly she wasn't.

Of course. They were in love with each other. The long nights out, the timing, the semitones of Cam's ambivalences and jealousies, even tonight's stupid perfect blazer and that last adjustment to his Disney curls and the speed of his walk.

But if it was true, why, in San Francisco, where men paraded naked and covered in glitter and nobody batted an eye, hadn't they figured it out and done something about it?

"You didn't know?" Mal asked, her head cocked to one side in curiosity that hadn't even a trace of sympathy in it. "I thought that was the attraction."

"I don't understand."

"It is for me. I know Will isn't going to want more from me than I'm willing to give."

"You don't want a relationship?"

Mal scoffed. "Not a chance." She went into the stall. From there, she said, while Laurie braced against the sink, "No more than you want one with Cam."

"Cam and I have been dating for a year."

"Sunk cost."

The sound of Mal flushing the toilet jarred Laurie's very bones. She wanted to storm out of the bathroom. Instead she stood transfixed while being casually stripped of certainties. And neither of the things she actually meant to say—*I love Cam*, or, *You don't know us*—would come out of her mouth.

"But Will's never expressed the slightest interest in men."

Mal washed her hands and shook them dry with careless finality. Raised an eyebrow in the mirror.

Maybe Laurie should have been defending Cam's heterosexuality instead? But she wasn't a liar, or a fool. She'd chosen to ignore the way Cam slept with his head on her chest instead of holding her to his. Chosen to feel relieved at the opportunity to offer comfort and support when he tearfully confessed that antidepressants had messed up his sex drive.

Chosen to forget what real attraction felt like.

"No, you're wrong," she said weakly.

"Let's find out," Mal said, and burst open the bathroom door.

Laurie had no choice but to follow, heart pounding.

"You took your time in there," Will said.

"Needed to get the lay of the land," Mal said, sitting down. "Besides, we wanted to give your stifled imaginations something to do." A flash of teeth; a smile like a whip. "What *must* we have been up to in there, just the two of us?"

"Not all men find the idea of two women titillating," Cam said, "especially not in San Francisco." He wasn't quite drawing himself up, but pulling back, freezing her out. Until that moment, Laurie had never seen it, now she couldn't stop wondering if he'd done it before, used Minnesota-nice feminism as a defensive weapon.

"Well, I find the idea of two men together to be an aphrodisiac," Mal said, snagging the last chip in the bowl. "And if you two weren't curious enough to try it, all your mescaline trips mustn't have taken you very far beyond your repressed Lutheran upbringing after all."

For a long beat, no one spoke. Laurie knew, of course. She knew from the way Cam refused to look at Will at all. From the small twitch at the end of Will's lips. All she could do was pray they'd all stay silent or change the topic.

A wide grin broke out on Mal's face. She turned to Will, open-mouthed. "*You popped his cherry.*"

Will shrugged. "It was college."

Laurie couldn't move. She was frozen, a perfect plastic smile plastered over the tumult in her gut that threatened to knock her down. She wanted to scream, but the same creature that had kept her from refusing these dinners now held her back from saying anything at all.

Cam's eyes turned to her—begging, terrified.

She held perfectly still, like a bug playing dead.

"Shall we get the bill?" Mal said.

"Yes," Will said, pulling her into his lap. "We've got to find a way to silence that troublesome mouth of yours."

"I can think of a few ways," Mal said, her dark pupils blown wide. She signaled the waiter and said, "I've got this. I can't stand the whole *Did you get one drink or two, we all shared the appetizer* crap. It's a taqueria."

"We usually split the bill," Cam said. The tip of his nose was white with fury.

"That doesn't seem fair," Mal said, and inserted a hundred-dollar bill into the black wallet the waiter held out to her. "Besides, I need change for cab fare."

Laurie's chest seized, and she coughed to take in a breath. After that—she was going to just *leave*.

Before she could say a word, Mal and Will were gone, whirling out of the taqueria with their hands all over each other, leaving her to pick up the pieces.

She grabbed her coat and walked out on unsteady legs.

"You look really gorgeous tonight," Cam said.

Of course she did. Choking on air that crackled with smoke from October's wildfires did wonders for the complexion.

He leaned in.

Fuck it.

"If you kiss me, you'll get hives," she said, and walked away.

chapter two

her name wasn't even Mal! As Vic's admin, Laurie filed the perfectly ordinary transfer request for a perfectly ordinary name—Malini Kumar—but nobody at the Unicorn used it. In tech, as in ancient times, important people only had one name, usually the one in their email handle. Vic was Vic@, and she was Mal. Although the way people said it, the woman might as well be Beyoncé.

First woman on the team, my ass.

Laurie herself had been first, but if you couldn't code you weren't a person. An admin might as well be furniture.

She decided to make herself some tea to shake off her mood. It had been a week since that disastrous dinner. Convention allowed her to grieve for at least three months for a year's relationship, but that sounded both exhausting and embarrassing. She hadn't realized she'd been administrating her relationship, anticipating Cam's needs and preventing catastrophe for so long that its arrival was actually a relief.

Her mother had always said, "Don't date a man prettier than you." She'd meant for Laurie to avoid New York's finance guys who demanded their girlfriends' thighs not touch and had a prenup clause about weight gain, not late-bloomers who might leave her hanging at forty to fuck their way across America, but the advice was sound.

What she missed most was how responsive Cam had been to her texts, but, as Vic was fond of saying, very loudly, on many occasions, "A bot can do that!" Who knew you could get withdrawal from the sound of a phone notification? It was worse than juvenile.

Tea it would have to be. Sober up like an adult. Someone here had to be one.

She braced when she saw Mal in the office kitchen, and remembered that Will was gone too. She asked Mal about him sympathetically, only to get a blank look and, "Why would I know how he's doing?"

"You aren't together anymore?"

"We never were. He invited me for the night, but he'd forgotten about that dinner with you and Cam, so he asked me to come along. Probably to get him out of it sooner."

All that effort... poor Cam.

"What's wrong?" Mal asked.

"Cam and I broke up." There. Said aloud for the first time.

"He wasn't right for you." Mal grabbed a protein bar and left her slack-jawed and stupidly holding a banana.

She didn't talk to Mal for a week. In the meantime, she had new problems. Her roommate had just moved out, and even if he'd frequently left the bathroom smelling of onion farts he paid his share of the rent on time. She spent her evenings interviewing people. Paystubs didn't guarantee sanity, and San Francisco's cray-cray could be anything from *You seemed stressed so I microdosed your granola,* to *You must have asked my other personality for the rent.*

The best candidate she'd found so far was a young woman who made a living as a photographer, capturing disconcerting closeups of the slow trickle of dew on fern and the sad faces of old men. Tatiana made a face when Laurie told her she worked at the Unicorn. Laurie figured you had to judge others' life-choices to feel better about your own. She'd resisted the urge to tell Tatiana to open a savings account.

That winter of 2007 felt precarious. Obama's star was on the rise and his implacable white-toothed smile said everything would get better, but the Dow was flickering, and Vic reeked of sweat as he convinced investors to hold steady through conference calls where they couldn't see the stains on his shirt.

"You should cash out," Mal said, coming up beside her at the company all-hands. "Any stocks or bonds, especially any real estate."

Laurie wanted to strangle her. As if she had any. Mal seemed unperturbed by the strange chaos of that year, when twenty-somethings kept private planes in swampy airfields along the Bay, while those old enough to be their parents huddled in tents that stank of urine along the Embarcadero. *Beware*, said their haggard, aged faces. *All this is temporary*, said their faux-Buddhist T-shirts. Long lines cued on either side of Valencia Street, five blocks from Laurie's house; on the one side, waiting for their social security paycheck, and on the other to pay thirty dollars for a breakfast sandwich and a glass of orange juice at Boogaloos.

Before she could say anything, Vic came up to them, throwing an arm around each of their shoulders.

"My two favorite people," he said, slurring slightly. "Why do you look so serious? And why aren't there drinks in your hands?"

Mal stepped away and said, "What can I get you?"

"Not a sh—shance," Vic said. "You're *my* team. My responsibility. My family." He snapped his fingers—who did that?—and a waiter came by with a tray of plastic wine glasses.

Mal reached for two glasses of red, and then one of her hands moved to a white, which she handed Laurie.

"How did—"

"Did you want the red?"

"No, but—"

"Mal, have you met Laurie?" Vic said. "She's… *so* amazing. She's organizing a ski trip to Tahoe for the whole team."

Laurie gave him a tense smile. He hadn't said, *She's so amazing for someone without a college degree*, but she always heard it anyway. Whatever. She'd been exceeding low expectations all her life.

"Really? A ski trip?" Mal asked.

"My friend Will has a place there, so—" Vic's eyes bulged comically—"You should stay with us! Both of you!"

"I'm booking us all rooms at the Hyatt," Laurie said, trying not to sound stressed. Last year's ski trip was where she'd met Cam, at Will's Tahoe house, but the team really didn't do well without adult supervision. The trip had meant one broken wrist, two concussions, and a bar brawl. While most drunk men overestimated their attractiveness, for some reason brilliant tech geniuses were prone to overestimating their proprioception and their bladder control, and she didn't want any trouble.

"Oh, you can bring your fiancé!" Vic turned to Mal to explain as if Laurie wasn't even there. "He's a serious, sysadmin type, you'd think he was no fun at all. But he's great once he's had a few drinks. Will knows how to get him to open up."

Mal grinned widely and opened her mouth. Before she could say something absolutely humiliating like *I bet he does*, Laurie said, "Cam's busy, but I'm sure he'll be thrilled you remember him."

"Well, then you have no excuse. You have to stay at the lodge with me and Will. Can't have two gorgeous girls moping on your own at the hotel, can we?"

He pinched her chin lightly, then stumbled away. Mal said nothing, but Laurie's ears burned, especially as those sharp eyes fell to the fake engagement ring she always wore to work.

"It's just…"

"Unwanted advances," Mal said, nodding. "But you'll need a new fake fiancé. He'll find out the truth as soon as he gets to Tahoe."

Just like that. No judgment, no outrage. Laurie was both relieved and unbearably exposed. As if by knowing about Vic and not doing or saying something about it she was responsible for his behavior. Complicit.

Now that Vic was gone, a few more daring young men came up to talk to them, or more accurately, to talk to Mal. Laurie understood nothing about version skew or confidence intervals, but these men were flirting, and the woman had no idea.

Mal, men don't ask women for advice on statistical problems.

"But let's talk about something else," Mal said. "Have you guys met Laurie? She sits in the corner office, under the Klimt print."

"That's not a real Klimt," Laurie said. "It's just a copy I made."

"You *made* that?"

"What's a Klimt?" someone asked.

"He's an artist," Laurie said, "and the painting is from the cover of a book I read once." She didn't want them asking about Vienna, where she'd never been.

Mal inhaled sharply, the full weight of her attention suddenly landing on her like a mallet. "You—I *knew* it. You were at Cornell, weren't you? In Professor H—'s class?"

Laurie hustled back to her desk without answering, feeling as if Mal's eyes were following her on a drone camera the whole way. Every time they met, Mal saw through her, unraveled some secret she'd meticulously tucked away, forced her to face the mirror.

But she had more immediate problems. By the time of the ski trip she was a nervous wreck. She'd interviewed only three applicants for the spare room, and the full rent was more than her monthly paycheck. The last thing she wanted was to go on the ski trip, but as the admin in charge of it she had no choice.

On the bus, someone said, "Seriously? *Beringer* chardonnay? We must be heading into a recession."

Laughter rolled through the seats. Tears pricked her eyes. Broke, to them, meant cheap wine and doubling up at four star hotels, not making a meal of peanut butter and onions or sharing a bathroom with a sweaty man who never cleaned the toilet.

Mal came up to the front of the bus, where Laurie sat just behind the driver. "I thought you might like some company. Aren't we supposed to be roommates?"

She still wasn't speaking to Mal, but they were the only two women on the team, so they had to room together. Mal seemed to take silence for acceptance, and sat down next to her.

"You and Cam," Mal whispered, "I've been meaning to ask. You didn't break up because of me, did you?"

Laurie didn't answer.

"Was it really a big deal? Lots of people are bisexual, you know."

God, she was so condescending. As if *that* was the issue.

"I just wish he'd told me," Laurie said. "Then I wouldn't be left wondering if I've been the consolation prize."

"He clearly wanted to be with you. Does it really matter if people's eyes wander from time to time, if they always come back to rest on you? Wouldn't you rather be chosen, over and over, than simply taken as a default?"

"That sounds soul-crushing. You must think I'm so bourgeois, expecting things like honesty and fidelity out of a relationship."

"The fact that you know what it means to be bourgeois means you aren't."

"And what about you?" Laurie asked. "Why were you so certain you didn't want to be with Will?"

"It's nothing to do with Will. I don't want to be with *anyone*. Why, in an age of birth-control and financial independence, would a woman compromise? No, lovers are like tapas meals, to be tasted without commitment."

"What about...?"

"Yes?"

"Love," she said. "What if you *wanted* to spend the rest of your life with someone?"

"Huh," Mal said, as if mulling over a new technical concept. "I suppose I wouldn't mind that, but I still wouldn't get *married* or anything. If you can't leave at any time, it's not love."

You don't know what it's like to be left.

They weren't yet past the snow line, and the pines outside the window looked just like the ones Laurie had left behind in the Adirondacks. She wondered if her mother and Jim were still getting along. She hadn't called in a while.

"So you think it's impossible to be in a relationship with someone without compromising?" she asked Mal.

"Not for very long."

"Huh," she said, just as Mal had. *But who are we outside of our relationships with other people?*

Ah—that was the true reason she was angry. Not at Mal, for exposing the truth. Not even at Cam, for hiding himself. Hadn't she done the same? To protect herself from Vic, to endear herself to Cam, to make herself comprehensible and competent. Where was the Laurie she'd once been, who walked against the current to feel the skin of the waterfall?

They arrived in Tahoe, and the crisp, cold air stirred her from a long, quiet wallow in thought. While talking to Mal felt like being in *The Matrix* and contorting to dodge bullets, in the silence afterwards she'd been combing through the debris and found no cartridges, no signs of the attack. She thanked the driver, directed people to the check-in desk, and made sure nobody had left anything on the bus.

"I can take your bags to our room," Mal said, holding out a hand.

Laurie hesitated.

"Or not," Mal said with a shrug. She didn't seem offended, but part of Laurie wanted to bring her up short, slow her down somehow. She was always moving forward into the next space, the next thought, without letting anyone prepare first.

"Wait." She passed Mal her suitcase. "Thank you."

Mal headed off.

It wasn't fair to keep holding Mal responsible for the end of her relationship. Laurie had hidden from the truth, made assumptions that Mal blasted with her roving, unpredictable gaze, like a park ranger clearing away squatters with a flashlight.

Night fell abruptly, within what felt like the span of an

exhale. The hot tubs, teeming with techies now, glistened like bioluminescence against the darkness. Nothing could compel Laurie to wear a bathing suit in front of her coworkers, but she wandered among them nursing a glass of champagne.

"... And then he just goes off to lunch, like he didn't just drop the damned database!"

Laughter. How strange, to hear words in her own language and not particularly understand them. To feel so visible, as a woman, and so invisible all at once.

When the cold burrowed through her flimsy coat, Laurie went inside to the card tables, and found Mal in the hotel's white robe, thumbing through a wad of bills. She rolled her eyes. Could she look more ridiculous, gambling in a bathing suit?

"There you are," Mal said, as if she'd been waiting for her. "Can you hold this? I don't have any pockets." She stuffed the money into Laurie's hand, letting a twenty-dollar bill float to the ground. Then she stumbled off, muttering, "Bathroom, wine, hot tub."

Laurie picked up the fallen twenty. She wanted to throw the money after her. Did Mal even know how much she'd given? Would she notice if Laurie kept it? She went upstairs to their room, annoyed that the hotel door wasn't built for slamming. She counted the bills. Nearly seven hundred dollars. Breathing hard, she stuffed it into Mal's backpack and sat down on the bed.

She should have gone after her, but had no idea what to say. She didn't even tell waiters when they brought her the wrong order, never mind how she'd articulate the strange, wandering anger that seemed to crawl beneath her skin now.

The ringing of a phone startled her so much she jumped out of the bed. Ah, Mal's phone. She ignored it and sat back down.

It rang again.

The phone was unlocked, so she answered in case it was Mal, lost and trying to call her phone to sort herself out.

"Hello?"

"Who's this?" demanded a woman's voice. "Where's Malini?"

"She's not here right now. Can I tell her who called?" (Admin reflexes).

"Where is she?"

"I can take a message."

"A message... a message, she says. Aditi's worried out of her mind, and Ashwin's called the police but they won't do anything. Listen, you tell my daughter to come home immediately. This isn't funny. If she doesn't call me back in twenty minutes, I'll—"

Laurie waited, holding the phone away from her ear, as if the woman's spittle could reach her from the other side. When there was nothing further, she said, "I'll let her know."

The call ended. She dropped the phone back into its nest of clothes like a snake. Unable to stand the thought of staying in the room, she headed back out to the hot tubs to find Mal.

From the balcony, she saw her sprawled against the edge of a tub, arms out to the sides. Mal's head lay back against the stone; her eyes were closed, and her long curly hair bounced gently on the bubbles by her chest. An empty plastic wine glass sat beside her outstretched hand.

By the time Laurie reached her, two men were helping Mal out of the tub. With her eyes half-closed, she leaned into them and muttered something Laurie couldn't make out.

"She's my roommate," Laurie said, heart pounding. "I can take her from here."

The men looked at each other. If they were part of Vic's team, she didn't recognize them in their bathing suits.

"You can't possibly carry her all the way."

Maybe she was paranoid. She really *couldn't* carry Mal, not even for a little while. But she couldn't leave her with them either.

"You can leave her here," she said. "She'll walk… eventually."

The men looked at each other again, then nodded and went away, leaving Mal sitting against the metal rung of the hot tub. Laurie breathed in and out slowly, letting the sounds of the men move away, until all she heard was the hot tub jets and her own breathing.

"Mal, wake up. Your mother called."

An annoyed groan was her only response.

Laurie placed her arm underneath Mal's and lifted her to her feet. It was slow going, but she did start walking, the cold air sobering her up a little.

"Two glasses of wine don't usually hit me this hard."

"How often have you had drinks at altitude?"

"First time," she said. "It's glorious."

Glorious wasn't the word Laurie would've used. Her nerves were pinched, and her mind tumbled out a rolling litany of worst-case scenarios. What if she falls down and breaks her head against the stone, what if she slips down the stairs, or has alcohol poisoning, or what if those men come back, what if this was her fault—

"Laurie, look." Mal came to a stop. Here, far from the steam and light of the hot tubs, she pointed to a clear sky over snowcapped mountains.

"Where's your robe?" Laurie asked, suddenly aware Mal was wearing just her bathing suit, a simple, sporty black piece that fitted her well without reaching or flattering, like an unvarnished truth.

"I'm not cold."

"That's because you're drunk."

"You tell my mother that?"

"Of course not. She wanted to know where you were, said someone had tried calling the police, but I didn't—Mal? Why are you laughing?"

"Because I did it. I really did it. I left. It's over, and I'm finally free."

Laurie swallowed. "Why don't you come inside and drink some water?"

Mal stopped laughing immediately. Her hand came up to pat Laurie on the head, nearly poking her eye out. "Sorry, I don't mean to scare you. I wasn't... being self-destructive. I was *celebrating*." With that, she turned to the mountains and gave a loud whoop.

Laurie gaped. She'd never heard a woman make a sound that loud. Certainly not like this, under the open, amplifying, public-use sky.

"What's the matter? Never heard a barb—barbaric yawp across the roofs of the world?"

Laurie burst into laughter. "You gave yourself hiccups. Okay, come in already, you can be just as untamed and untranslatable inside. Also, I'm freezing, even if you aren't."

Mal stumbled along and then came to a sudden stop. "Untranslatable," she whispered. "That's it, exactly. That's how I feel, all the time."

"I was just—"

"I know what you were doing," Mal said, her eyes skewering Laurie as if she were a butterfly on the head of a pin. "You're *extremely* well-read. Most people would have thought I was quoting *Dead Poets Society*, and that's if they'd thought anything at all."

All Laurie's worry and irritation left her in a dizzying swoop, as she had the unfamiliar sensation of allowing herself to hear praise as praise. Not as reproach, or as the opening to ask a favor. After years of the tech equivalent of 'Don't worry your pretty little head about it' from the Unicorn's engineers, being truly seen felt like the prickle of hot water after being out too long in the numbing cold.

She went to fill a cup with water from the tap when they got to the room, but when she came out Mal was already drinking from the water bottle by the minibar. Laurie bit down on the itch to tell her it wasn't covered by the corporate card. Everything in the Unicorn's office kitchens was free, including the soy milk and the vitamin water that were supposed to regulate stress and boost brain function. There were times Will had walked out of restaurants without paying, unused to waiting for a bill.

Maybe a day would come when Laurie's eyes saw an item before its price tag, but it wasn't today.

"I've been trying to move out of my sister's house for a year," Mal said. "Each time I tried, something got in my way. When I started looking for apartments, my mother asked me if I hated my family so much I'd waste money on my own place. I tried to keep my evenings for myself, but my sister begged me to spend time with my niece. When I wanted to buy a car, my brother-in-law insisted on driving me everywhere. At some point, I couldn't take it. I went home after work with Will, and didn't come back until the next evening."

"I take it that ended badly."

"You could say that. They blindsided me. Invited over a family friend whose son might make me a good husband."

"I didn't think people still did that," Laurie said. "I'm assuming you refused."

"If only it was that simple. They don't just make you feel bad about refusing, they make you feel *wrong*. Do you have any idea how humiliating it is for the girl's family to refuse an alliance like that? How could you *possibly* want to live alone, when you could be surrounded by love? Why would you drive on the 101 yourself when you have a brother-in-law so devoted he'd drop anything to take you where you needed to go and it would be faster in the carpool lane?"

"Why do they think you've run away?"

"Because I have." Mal got up and spread her arms to encompass the backpack and its spilled contents. "Passport, credit cards, phone, laptop and three sets of clothes. Oh, and a bathing suit. What more does anyone really need?"

Laurie frowned. "But where will you live? When we head back, I mean."

"I'll check into a hotel near the office. I'm sure I'll find an apartment in a few days."

The phone rang again.

"Aren't you going to answer it?"

"Why?"

She opened her mouth to respond, but had no ready answer. It was unfathomable to Laurie to *not* pick up a ringing phone, or to leave one place without having another to spend the night. She ought to tell Mal she was looking for a roommate, that all this felt like some goofy, overdone footwork by the fates. But the thought of Mal walking through her apartment felt too intimate. Mal would know even more about her than she already did, and she wouldn't be silent about it either. Laurie needed a roommate who was stupider, more self-absorbed.

Then again, what if Mal found out from someone else that she'd been looking for a roommate? Laurie had posted pictures in the work chatrooms. Maybe Mal already knew. Maybe Mal had mentioned the hotel to spare Laurie the sting of rejecting her shitty place.

Before she could make sense of her thoughts, Mal had slipped into the shower. Steam seeped out from underneath the door.

The phone rang two more times before Mal came out, and each time Laurie's fingers itched to answer. The sound was like a baby's cry, wrenching and urgent, short-circuiting every other thought. It was always *her* mother at the other end, sobbing as she told Laurie her father was dead.

"I should change my number," Mal said, coming out wrapped in a towel. She turned off the phone so it would stop ringing, and sat down on the bed. "Shall I order us a pizza?"

Laurie hadn't noticed she was ravenous. "Don't worry about it."

"If *I* order a veggie pizza, will you eat some?"

"Maybe a slice."

When Mal didn't say anything, Laurie turned to look. She was dialing room service from the hotel phone. Mal put in the order and then said, as if there had been no break in the conversation, "We're not so different, you know. Neither of us wants to be helped by other people. Too many strings attached."

It wasn't *exactly* the same. She doubted Mal had ever had a sibling call her from jail after being caught selling marijuana. Or that she'd ever had to listen politely to the dangers of the gay agenda to get cheap furniture at a garage sale. But maybe they did both know what it was to be disappointed by those they loved.

Tatiana might make a great roommate, plastering the walls with enormous prints of her photographs. One day, she'd get a proposal from a curator interested either in her or her art, and she'd leave Laurie with a pitying look and a deep sense of the life she could've lived. Or she might be a terrible roommate, scattered artist mind and rent never paid on time and the faint scent of mold concealed by the stronger smell of turpentine.

"You could stay with me," Laurie said, "until you find another place."

chapter three

Sure: the word with which Mal accepted her offer, without bothering to negotiate the rent.

What had Laurie expected? It was an apartment, not a grand gesture. An ordinary Victorian where they quickly formed a cautious coexistence with the mice in the walls and commiserated about the poor insulation on colder nights.

Everything was fine, except for that *Sure*—it was *everywhere*.

Can you take out the garbage? *Sure.*

Do you mind splitting the HBO subscription? *Sure.*

As if splitting chores and bills wasn't a requirement of cohabitation but a favor Mal was granting her. The first time they went in to work together on the BART, Laurie turned to say something—just as Mal stuffed in earphones and closed her eyes to catch a little more sleep.

They didn't come home together. Mal went out drinking with the guys. She'd invited Laurie once, but they'd talked shop the whole time and Laurie was reminded of being sent to the kitchen while the men watched the game. Now she stayed home, painting tulips and redbuds and crabapple trees from memory, or reading a bodice ripper that made her wonder why she'd put up with bad sex as long as she had.

Mal wasn't deliberately inconsiderate. She simply lived in her own world, bent over her laptop screen or lost in a book, so the ordinary concerns of the world rarely reached her. A month into living together, a lightbulb in the kitchen started to flicker. When Laurie asked Mal about it, she said, "Oh, it's been doing that all day."

"Why didn't you change it?"

Mal gave her a blank stare. "Where do we keep spare bulbs?"

"In the closet over the washer. Could you get one?"

"Sure."

Laurie bit her lip and considered her words. "I could use help taking care of this place. It's hard to clean under the tub, and I can't reach the bookshelves."

"I'll take care of it," Mal said.

Two days later, Laurie came home to find a small, squat Latina woman standing on a chair and vigorously waving a feather duster over the bookshelves.

Sneezing, she knocked on Mal's door and entered to find her reading on her mattress. She hadn't bothered to buy a bed. She picked from a small bowl of almonds by her side on the floor, like a Roman emperor.

"Who's that?" Laurie asked.

Mal grinned, looking entirely too impressed with herself. "I found a house cleaner from the immigrant labor collective. Isn't she great? Her name's Dolores. She'll be here once a week."

"What's her rate?"

"I'll take care of it," Mal said, again.

Laurie was thinking up non-passive-aggressive I-statements that might help clarify the issue with just hiring a house-cleaning service without talking to her, when Mal lifted her head out of the book. "Oh, I meant to ask, are you going to Nick's party tonight?"

"Are you?"

"I have a date."

Laurie's eye twitched. "The guy from the Symphony?"

Mal had taken her there soon after they moved in together, offered the extra ticket casually, as if she could easily find someone else to take it if Laurie refused. Mal had no idea what music meant to her. Of course, once they were there, someone caught her eye and she left with him after the concert while Laurie took the BART home alone.

Mal made a face. "No, he tasted like cigarettes. Such a disappointing crash. One minute, we're listening to Tchaikovsky, the next we're kissing in an alley that smells like piss while he tells me he's allergic to latex."

A smile tugged at Laurie's lips. "Nobody ever lives up to the imagination, do they?"

"I met tonight's guy in line at Bluebottle," Mal said. "I have no expectations beyond a good taste in coffee."

"I wonder if that heightens or lowers a man's anxiety, to know you need nothing from him."

"I think any guy who wants me to need him is barking up the wrong tree," Mal said with a smile. "I refuse to need people I can't pay. That's exploitation."

Laurie turned to go, a sudden prickling in her gut telling her to leave before this conversation cut any deeper.

• • •

Nick's house was at the top of a hill in the Castro, and as Laurie climbed she watched cars struggle up the steep incline in fear and trembling, as if they might be struck down by a vengeful heterosexual god.

She milled around the crowd of jeans-and-hoodie techies holding a red plastic cup full of fancy white wine—leftovers from a work summit she'd organized. The men ignored her in favor of lounging on their bean bags to play video games, so she wandered through the house pretending to look for a friend, when a woman walked in wearing a dark-rose leather bandage dress with Gucci heels, promptly creating a center of gravity around herself unlike anything Laurie had ever seen.

"Ah, Sophia's here," Nick said, without looking up from his video game. "Only two hours late this time."

The woman in question knelt beside him and gave him a kiss on the cheek.

"Hey Nicky."

She didn't wait for him to acknowledge her, but instead got up from the ground without touching her hands to the floor, a feat of quad strength Laurie could only marvel at. Sophia went into the kitchen and proceeded to fit an entire taco laden with guacamole into her bow-lipped wine-red mouth while a dozen people watched her like a reality TV show.

"*That's* your ex?" someone asked Nick.

"When she was straight," he said. "Pre-IPO."

The other guy whistled.

Laurie went into the kitchen, suddenly aware of the fact that all her clothes had come from the thrift store. Sophia's eyes landed on her, and she blushed all the way down to her chest.

"You're new," Sophia said.

"I'm Laurie. I work with Nick."

"You're far too cute for this crowd."

She couldn't say a word. She hadn't known attraction could

feel like this, a wild and uncontrollable nausea that made her want to throw up or run away. She dashed out of the kitchen before she could embarrass herself, but no matter where she went, she couldn't seem to keep Sophia out of her peripheral vision.

The round of video games ended with shouts of triumph and despair, and the bean bags were cleared. Some pop hit started to play out of a network of wall-mounted speakers, and Sophia took the middle of the dance floor. She danced in Nick's arms, her back against his chest, content to be held there.

"Lucky dog," someone muttered. Laurie knew better. There were few things as torturous as staying close to someone who wasn't actually yours. Sophia was using Nick, as if he were a parking space she wanted to make sure stayed available.

Maybe the bitter burn in her stomach was something else altogether.

The song ended, and Sophia broke Nick's embrace. "Oh my God, is it already ten? I need to head out."

"I guess you wouldn't be *you* unless you had to get to at least three parties on a Saturday night," Nick said.

"Robyn's only in town for this weekend. I haven't seen her since South by South West last year."

Sophia started making her way to the exit, saying goodbyes to an endless line of awkward men whose names she botched with endearing abandon.

"Wait, Robyn?" someone asked Nick. "Isn't that the girl she left you for?"

Laurie went to Nick's bedroom, where she'd left her coat. She interrupted two people in a make-out session, apologized more for her own discomfort than theirs (they didn't seem to care), and put on her puffy coat. It was probably as red as her face and made her look like a skewered apple. She didn't say goodbye, since she doubted anyone had noticed her presence. She ran to the MUNI stop and saw Sophia standing there, staring into the light of her phone, annoyed.

"Everything okay?"

Sophia looked up. Laurie immediately regretted asking. It was ingrained in her to help.

"I don't suppose you want to go to another party? Robyn's plastered, and she'll get awfully clingy if I seem unattached."

Laurie wanted to say that she probably wasn't dressed right for Sophia's kind of party, but the words that actually came out of her mouth were, "Would she believe someone like you was with someone like me?"

Sophia frowned. Then she touched Laurie's cheek, quickly and tenderly.

"Oh, kitten," Sophia said, and kissed her.

Laurie froze at the electric tingle on her lips.

"Yeah, you're coming with me," Sophia said as the MUNI arrived.

They went to a nondescript building in SoMa where a warehouse had been converted into a club with high ceilings. Along the walls were a number of king beds, with the warehouse center cleared to allow an aerialist to perform acrobatics on a silk rope.

"White sheets?" Sophia said. "We *are* living on the edge." She led Laurie to a bed where three women were sitting with their backs against the wall. Each of them was lovely in that unreal doll-like way of Marina and Los Angeles girls, and Laurie soon discovered Robyn was the one with waist-length blonde curls and legs so long they glowed like gunmetal in thigh-high leather boots.

A waiter came by with tiny pieces of sourdough and caviar and a bottle of wine. One of the other women on the bed shifted slightly to show more skin, but if the waiter noticed he didn't so much as twitch in response.

"You're cute," Robyn said. "Not Soph's usual type, but then who is."

"That's a beautiful corset," Laurie said, desperate for something to say.

"Do you like it?" Robyn asked, preening. "I only got it today. Soph, she likes the corset. You'll have to get her one."

Sophia's eyes went dark. She pulled Laurie away from Robyn's grasp and into her lap.

The aerialist appeared, wearing what appeared to be a sequined bathing suit. She stroked herself with the silk fabric that hung from the ceiling, then easily climbed the rope to dangle upside-down from about fifteen feet in the air.

Sophia sighed against her back, putting one arm around Laurie's waist. With the other, she fed her some of her own wine.

"It's just a sad imitation of Paris," Robyn said. "Soph, remember that night in Montmartre with the chocolatier?"

Laurie smiled. It was awkward, clear, understandable, Robyn's lunge at a shared memory—it wasn't unlike Cam's attempts to pull rank over her with Will, an older friend asserting their territory. A sad imitation of intimacy. She didn't mind. After all, this was all just a show.

"Hm," was all Sophia offered.

"I don't know how you can stand this city," Robyn said. "A bunch of suddenly rich schoolboys who can't meet your eyes, and innocent Midwestern girls who call the city *San Fran* and think they're suddenly cultured because they're drinking red wine out of a bottle, not a box."

Sophia pulled Laurie's head back onto her shoulder and kissed her bared throat.

"Look at how responsive you are," Sophia said, seeing her skin blaze. "We're going to have so much fun together, aren't we kitten?"

Sophia's arms came up around her, pulling her into a cuddle. Inexplicably, Laurie relished the obvious jealousy on the other women's faces. She wasn't usually like this. As a child she'd once stopped running in a race because the other kids seemed to want the candy more. But then there was that flash of memory from the Symphony—a predatory grin, a spark in Mal's eyes, a conspiring whisper, before she left Laurie's side: *Want. Take. Have.*

"San Francisco has its perks," Sophia said, and kissed her right over her hammering heart.

• • •

The next few weeks were a reckless dream. There were parties in the Haight where the boys dressed in tutus and glittered stockings, and the girls wore leather or nothing at all. Sophia, it turned out, worked not for a Unicorn but for a stock market Darling, a tech company that had already started trading publicly, turning twenty-somethings into overnight millionaires.

They no longer had to work, any of them, but they chose to anyway, driven to *mean* something, to not let their newfound wealth grind down their souls. So they wore Swarovski on their feet and earrings made of recycled CDs; they bought VIP tickets to concerts to have the kind of backstage intercourse with the band that involved a discussion of lyrics rather than sex. They drove back from Hearst Castle arguing animatedly about the aesthetics of a Greek outdoor pool or a Roman indoor bath, then plunged, high and laughing, into the ocean at Half Moon Bay.

Laurie never told Mal about any of it, and if her roommate noticed the dark circles around her eyes or the residual glitter that clung to their hardwood floors despite Dolores' efforts, she never said anything. Laurie resented Mal's lack of curiosity as much as she dreaded having to tell her at some point. Would Mal have judged her? Probably not, but that was another kind of problem: she'd understand and accept her actions when Laurie couldn't yet. She was still swirling in the sweat and sparkle of those weeks.

Right before the office holiday parties that would close out the year, in the changing room of Dark Garden, she struggled with the corset Sophia had chosen for her. It was delicately boned in the lightest blush-pink, but as she tried to figure out the hooks and ribbons she came across the price-tag and her mind went white.

"I'm coming in!" Sophia called, walking past the velvet curtain.

Laurie clutched the corset over her chest.

"Don't be shy. Let me help."

She handed it to Sophia, who undid the lacing and stood behind her, wrapping the bone. Laurie held the front in place, gasping when the ribbon pulled too tight.

"God, look at you," Sophia said. "We have to get this."

"We can't. It's almost eight hundred dollars. Where would I wear it? And I don't have anything to wear it *with*."

"Shh," Sophia said. "What have I always said about money?"

"That nothing turns you on more than destroying it in the service of beauty."

She was dead serious about that. She'd told Laurie her fantasy, that she wanted to love someone so much that she'd run to them through the mud, Manolo Blahnik heels be damned. As far as Laurie was concerned, if you knew that you were the kind of impulsive person who might end up running in mud or fainting in the grass, you had no business buying the kind of heels that might mean broken ankles, but she knew better than to say anything. Among the Darlings, she was the crazy one for seeing something wrong with Agent Provocateur lingerie in the dryer or nacho crumbs on the Ligne Roset couch.

Something niggled at her, beyond the talk of money, like a mouse in the corner of her vision. Sophia never kissed her in front of her techie friends. When they went to DNA lounge, they danced as a group. Laurie wanted to ask: *Would you run through the mud for me?*

She said instead, "You don't have to do this. I'd be just as happy staying home."

"I want everyone to see you," Sophia said. "And *I* want to see you in the satin gown I got you, knowing you're wearing this corset... and *nothing* but this corset underneath. And when my idiot colleagues inevitably end the evening by stumbling into you with a plastic cup of cheap beer, I'll take you home and rip the dress off you before we're even out of the limo."

Laurie's skin kept no secrets, but at the image Sophia wove she started shaking, unable to get enough air with the corset on.

"You're overwhelmed, aren't you, kitten," Sophia said, stroking her hot cheek. "Let me help."

Those three words were enough, always, to turn her mind blank and her body pliant. They were a comfort, taking away hard decisions about what she ought to say or do to hold Sophia's interest, cutting past anxieties about how much she'd spent on her. *Let me help* meant letting Sophia dress and undress her, touch her, kiss her, spoil her, possess her completely.

chapter four

One Sunday morning, Laurie came home to Lakmé. If she thought it strange to hear the Léo Delibes opera from behind Mal's door, there weren't words for the terror she found in the tub: dark rivulets of red everywhere. She thought Mal had cut herself and tried to bleed out.

She ran to Mal's bedroom and threw open the door, only to find her roommate standing half-naked in the center of her room amidst a pile of clothes. Mal wore plain black underwear and a sports bra that flattened her chest. Her hands were on her hips, and she turned to Laurie, a contemplative look on her face.

"Oh, hello. You're home earlier than usual."

Laurie skipped past the fact that Mal evidently knew she wasn't spending the nights at home and asked what the hell happened to the bathroom.

"I was going to clean it up. I tried to dye my hair." Mal undid a knot and her curls fell over her shoulders. "It was an utter failure. I think I need to get it done professionally."

Her laptop was now playing the Flower Duet, when Lakmé and her servant Mallika wander off to gather flowers by a river. Did Mal know that it was this duet that had first allowed

Laurie to understand that women stirred her in a way that men never could?

"It's beautiful, isn't it?" Mal said.

"Since when do you listen to opera?"

"I don't. I was just feeling nostalgic. I fell in love with the Flower Duet in college." Mal eyed her carefully and added, "I studied it in the class where I first saw you."

Nope. Not going there. "I'll let you get back to... whatever you were doing."

"You could stay. Help me pick out an outfit for the holiday party."

"Well, you've got to start with better underwear. You can't wear formal wear over an athletic bra."

Mal made a face. "I don't suppose you've any time today to help me shop?"

Actually, Laurie couldn't think of anything better than not having the attention on herself for a while. Sophia had been texting constantly, planning their hair and makeup for the party—"It's NARS or nothing"—as if the boys weren't going to show up in T-shirts and sneakers.

Who are we dressing for?

They headed to the Nordstrom on Market Street to get Mal fully outfitted, where the lingerie ladies gave what Laurie had recently come to understand was their standard lecture to women who'd never been fitted for a bra (most women). They left her with a range of DD bras and a lecture on the long-term consequences of LuluLemon.

"You'd think I slapped their children," Mal muttered.

"Amazing how many people you can offend without even trying. Imagine if you were trying," Laurie said. She hadn't meant anything by it, but maybe it sounded like an accusation.

"I didn't mean—"

"I think you just proved your own point," Mal said, smiling.

That was it? No drama?

They moved on to the formal wear section. Being on this side of the equation was far better, although it was all Laurie could do to keep from laughing at Mal's truly awful taste. First it was a strapless orange number that squashed her breasts, then a shiny golden babydoll outfit that made her look like a drag queen.

"What do you think of this?"

Laurie grimaced.

"No?" Mal asked. "But it's red. Everyone's supposed to be able to wear red."

"It's wearing you."

"Savage. And they say I'm the bossy one."

Mal grinned and went back into the changing room without waiting for her reply.

Laurie's stomach tugged in sympathy. They did call Mal the bossy one. To a team that had never had a guiding hand, even the slightest management was the height of oppression. Maybe they just found it galling that Mal was younger than most of her subordinates. Laurie had even had to find time for some of them to complain to Vic about her. But Vic, for all his flaws, knew when Mal was right. It was how he treated Mal that showed Laurie how little he respected her.

The mouse, again, at the periphery of her vision. She'd once pointed out to Sophia that vermilion was in the orange family, warmer than crimson, which came from the carmine family. Sophia had moved onto the next topic as if Laurie hadn't spoken at all.

"I hate this," Mal said, breaking her out of her reverie.

"What if I picked something out for you?"

"Would you?"

She found Mal a few things to try on, hoping she'd see what Laurie saw. Mal was a force of nature, so only natural or jewel tones would suit. No patent leather, no artifice. Autumn colors would set off her dark skin without turning her into something she wasn't.

She waited outside the changing room to give Mal some privacy. To fill in the silence, she asked, "Who are you going with, anyway?"

"You, of course," Mal said. "I assume you have your ticket, since you're the one who gave me mine."

"I have an errand to run first, so I might be a little late. Aren't you bringing a date?" She hadn't told Mal, or anyone, that she wasn't planning on going. Sophia's office party was on the same night, and Vic would have a jealous fit if he knew she was choosing to party with the Darlings over his Unicorn. Besides, as long as she put in a quick appearance for Vic, she didn't think anyone else at work would notice she wasn't there the whole time.

"A date?" Mal said. "No. Wouldn't want anyone to get the wrong idea."

"What idea?"

Mal opened the door, and Laurie's mouth went dry. The halter of the forest-green dress hung so low that the inches of cleavage made it impossible to look away from Mal's chest. Her dark, brown arms were toned, and between them and her too-long legs, her peerless skin seemed to go on without limit.

"That they have a shot at something long-term," Mal said. "I don't want to lead anyone on."

Damn her to hell.

• • •

The Darling held their 2007 holiday party on the San Francisco pier, after converting a collection of interconnected warehouses into a "world-tour." *One World* was the theme, celebrating the globalization that had made them the stock market favorite they were, and so waitresses wore saris in one room and kimonos in another, while Sophia and Laurie stepped out of a limo to be greeted by a half-naked satyr covered in bronze body-paint and artificial grapes.

In the *Middle East* room—"Well, what else would you call it? It's time people got over their nationalist bullshit, don't you think?"—belly dancers performed for an awestruck audience, while servers brought them cinnamon-dappled hot wine. Laurie trailed behind Sophia as she whirled through room after room of simplified, stereotyped geopolitics, glad that nobody paid any attention to her in the slipstream.

Eventually, she left to find the bathroom and took her place in a long, growing line.

"Fifty bucks on cousin," said the woman in front to her friend, nodding at a statuesque woman in a miniskirt and six-inch heels a few feet away.

"I'm not taking that bet. The C cup says cousin, but the ass is all escort. That butt is at least three thousand bucks."

The women laughed and turned to Laurie.

"What's your bet?" one of them said.

"My... bet?"

"We saw a dozen Craigslist ads for dates to this party last night alone. Around midnight the going rate was five thousand an hour."

"Just to be a date, mind you," the other clarified. "Strictly no sex."

Her shock must have shown, because the first woman said, "Didn't you know?"

Laurie shook her head.

"I'm Alyssa."

"And I'm Brandi."

"Laurie."

"So, you're Sophia's girlfriend," said Brandi. "We saw you enter through Greece."

"She doesn't like that word, remember?" Alyssa said. "Partner, S.O., something gender-neutral. Less heteronormative."

They shared a laugh.

"Are you friends of hers?" Laurie asked.

The women looked at each other, as if silently debating something.

"Sophia doesn't have female friends," Alyssa said. "And the only male ones she has are her exes."

Laurie shook her head. Sophia wasn't just a party animal; she *was* the party.

"Listen, kid," Brandi said, "Sophia has the attention span of a butterfly. And she's too smart and too damn rich to tie up her assets in a marriage that could ruin her financially. So if you want to enjoy this as long as you can, stay pretty but not too pretty."

"And save up for the day she gets bored," Alyssa added.

The women turned away and the line for the bathroom inched forward.

Maybe she should have left the line and waited over at one of the other bathrooms. But Laurie couldn't move. Their words festered. She'd been at the party for almost two hours but

Sophia had yet to introduce her as a girlfriend. She wracked her memory for any other time in the last several weeks when Sophia had introduced her to anyone.

This is Laurie.

You have to meet Laurie.

Laurie, Pablo. You both love Neko Case.

No, she didn't need to worry. After all, she hadn't introduced Sophia to anyone either. Besides, what was it Mal had said? That it *meant* something to be invited to a holiday party.

I don't want to lead anyone on.

What was she even doing? She and Sophia couldn't marry. What if Sophia got tired of her when she was forty, or fifty, when she couldn't work the same punishing hours, and her looks couldn't find her a husband with health insurance?

Laurie glared at her reflection in the mirror. She was wearing too much makeup, like a child going through her mother's things. No wonder Alyssa and Brandi hadn't taken her seriously.

"Are you okay?"

"I can't…" She clutched the edge of the sink.

Alyssa's hand came to rest on her back. "Bran, help me get this corset off her. It's too tight. She can't breathe."

In the mirror, she could see a crowd collecting behind her. She wanted to cry, to tell them not to take off the corset, that she'd get herself under control. She just needed them to stop *staring*.

Alyssa and Brandi pulled her into the large accessible stall and locked it behind them. That was better. Fewer people. Still, here she was, hyperventilating among strangers like a child lost at a supermarket.

The dress came off first, leaving her in just her corset and heels. As soon as the top laces came off, she drew in a large, gulping breath and started to cry. "Please, a tissue. I don't want to stain it."

It wasn't as if Sophia would say anything, but she couldn't bear the thought of getting wet mascara on the corset.

"I'm sorry," she said. "I feel like an idiot."

Brandi squatted down so their eyes were level. "I'm guessing Sophia's your first real girlfriend."

"I've dated people before."

"There's a big difference between *dating people* and being in a relationship," Brandi said, her arms folded.

"And women hit different," Alyssa said. "I don't know why, but it's the truth. Maybe you think the only way someone really gets inside you is physically so you're not expecting it when they flay you to the bone. Or maybe you expect more, because you think someone who has a car of their own should be a better driver."

Brandi tried to pull her into a hug, but Laurie resisted. "I'll ruin your dress."

"Shut up."

Brandi yanked her into a warm hug, where, embarrassed and exhausted beyond endurance, she started sobbing. "I'm so sorry. I'm ruining your party."

"Eh, it's not really a party until someone's vomiting or crying," Brandi said.

Eventually Laurie pulled her phone out of her purse. She'd promised to meet Sophia in the Italy room nearly half an hour ago.

There were no missed calls or messages.

"A butterfly," Brandi said, putting her arm around Alyssa's waist. "Take it from us. You want the kind of woman who'll watch bad soap operas with you, not the one who wants to star in them herself."

"Everyone thinks they're the main character these days," Alyssa grumbled, shaking her head sadly.

Laurie let them retie the corset, although not as tightly as before—"you have nice enough tits without giving yourself a mammogram"—and slid into the white satin gown, noticing for the first time how her own hips were much wider than Sophia's, even as Alyssa said, "She won't get bored of you. She'll hate you for being prettier first."

She meant to argue, but they were already on their way out. Laurie went over to the Italy room, where Styrofoam blocks were set up to look like Roman ruins. A bright blue pool in the middle spit out bubbles and steam. Around the pool, men took off their silk suits and jumped in, while bored staff in togas handed towels to the few shrieking women who seemed to have jumped in, cocktail dress and all.

Sophia sat at the top of a makeshift wall, a heeled foot dangling precariously over the pool. She leaned back against a fake Doric column, her eyes half-closed. The thin strap of her dress had come loose on one side, falling to the arm that held a wine-glass. She held court, with several men sitting around her and hanging on her every word.

"Laurie!" Sophia cried out. "Come here. I was just telling the guys about you."

Laurie took her place at her side, glad of the way Sophia's arm made its way around her waist, possessive and affectionate.

Girlfriend. Partner. Significant other.

The words passed through her mind as she considered introducing herself next time instead of waiting for Sophia to do it.

"Okay, I take it back," one of the guys said. "Now that I see her, she's nothing like I imagined."

"Oh? What did you imagine?" Laurie asked. "What's Sophia been saying about me?"

"Nothing that isn't true," Sophia said. "You're a great dancer, you work ridiculous hours for criminally low pay, and you always know the right thing to say to everyone."

"And that you're an artist," the guy said, something lewd and eager in his gaze that made Laurie's hair stand on end. "She said you've painted a few nudes of her."

It was one thing to be accounted for as a girlfriend, a partner, a significant other. An equal. Yes, there was the implication of sex in that relationship, but there was something that didn't quite sit right about the idea that Sophia was telling these strangers, men, about something Laurie considered more intimate than sex. She had slept with a few people. She'd only ever painted Sophia.

"Someday when I'm old and gray those paintings will be worth millions," Sophia said.

"You're not going to sell them!" she said, suddenly frightened. She wasn't really an artist. It would be humiliating to have her art critiqued by professionals, who would see every amateur stroke.

Ignoring her, Sophia leaned over to whisper to the guy, placing an arm on his shoulder for support. The strap of her dress fell aside, so the guy had a full view of her chest as she said, "I'm just lucky she doesn't know her own worth. If she ever actually put her artistic talents out there, she'd be a millionaire and she wouldn't have any more use for me!"

Laurie bit her lip hard. Sophia's vision of her scraped hard against the edges of memories she'd never shared with anyone, images that crowded into her mind now, unasked for and insistent—being packed into a car in the middle of the night to drive to another state, her mother crying with relief the day they found out her father had finally died. There was a particular kind of furious hurt that came from loving someone who didn't just refuse to be loved but took pleasure in *punishing* those who dared challenge their cynical worldview by loving them at all.

"I love you, Sophia Melnyk," she said, pulling her close. "Not just when you're dressing me up like a doll or when you're taking me to fancy clubs and parties. I love how you know all the lyrics to every Decemberists song, and how even the fanciest sushi doesn't make you as happy as a McDonald's burger, and I'll still love you when you have wrinkles and gray pubes. Okay?"

It could have been a moment. Maybe if they'd been alone. If they'd been older.

Instead, Sophia pulled away. "You're so cute," she said. And then she pushed Laurie into the water.

When she rose to the surface, there was laughter everywhere. The white satin gown was sodden through, the bone of the corset now visible to all. Trembling, Laurie made her way to the edge of the pool and climbed out of the water, aware of all the eyes on her body. A staff member with a stiff expression handed her a towel.

Without looking back, ignoring Sophia's half-hearted apologies, she picked up her coat from the coatcheck and got in a waiting taxi.

"Going home already?" the driver said, giving her a pitying glance in the rearview mirror.

She looked out of the window so he'd stop speaking to her. It was a tactic she'd learned from the techies who did it to her. They passed the curved triangles of the Bay Bridge, lit up like arcs of hope and despair. She'd come to this city over that bridge, taken the bus from Emeryville after three days on the California Zephyr because she couldn't afford to fly. Eaten an apple and a bag of potato chips every day, rationing out the latter so it would turn into dinner.

She'd taken this exact route then, her heart expanding a couple of sizes at the sight of the rainbow flags in the Castro. She'd fallen in love hard, despite having only enough money to afford a couch covered in cat hair. That year, she danced in the street on Halloween to Eurythmics, happy to belt out that sweet dreams were made exactly of this. Stumbled home one night at 3 AM and met Telopa, an artist who insisted on sketching her. He lit up when she recognized he was painting in the Mannerist style, and asked her, "Why isn't life always like this? Just filled with random acts of artistic kindness?"

She was nearly home, but she wasn't going to let her night end like this. This was *her* city. Her mind sought out the dress she'd originally wanted to wear. She'd got it for thirty dollars at the thrift store near Cam's house. That district—Pacific Heights, or more colloquially, Specific Whites—always had the best hand-me-downs. She'd tried it on during her post-Cam house cleaning, when she and Mal were still finding their way around each other.

"One of the benefits of having a woman roommate is I can now bother you with that age-old question: do you think this dress makes my ass look big?" she'd said wryly, not expecting an answer.

Mal leaned against the doorway, her head to the side, assessing. "Yes, but that's a feature not a bug, isn't it?"

"Out," Laurie had said, too shocked to do anything but laugh. "Why am I even asking you?"

The cab stopped. It wasn't even nine o' clock. If she

hurried, she could still change her outfit and make it to the Unicorn party.

. . .

As soon as she entered the restaurant she'd booked out for the Unicorn's party, Laurie felt better. Theirs was a more restrained extravagance, a pre-IPO tightrope where frugality would shake investor confidence but frivolity would frighten them more. No satyrs, no belly dancers. Instead these executives drank Moët Chandon straight out of the bottle, while their engineers made faces at the foie gras but valiantly ate it anyway.

She found Mal making conversation with the crowd of men who always hovered around her like fruit flies, and walked over. Were those—yes, they really were gold-buckled cowboy boots on her feet. A stark, but not entirely awful, contrast to the lovely green dress, and reassuringly stable after all those escorts in pencil heels at the Darling party.

"Only you would wear a cocktail dress with boots," Laurie said.

Mal smiled widely, and the circle of people expanded to let her in. "Laurie! I wasn't going to last four hours in heels." She dusted off the ruffles on the dress. "Besides, I looked a bit too much like foliage."

A ripple of laughter went through the crowd.

As if drawn in by the sound, Vic came up to them, throwing an arm around Laurie and the man beside her, draping himself over them both like a tablecloth. The arm around her held the neck of a champagne bottle. "Laurie! You're finally here. Now it's a party. Why are you always empty-handed? It's criminal is what it is." He looked around at the men. "Why the hell are you just standing there? Where are your manners? Get these girls something to drink!"

"It's all right, Vic," she said, but the men had already dispersed, scrambling to obey.

"It's not," Vic said, slurring his words. "I heard about you and Cam. It's awful. You know you can talk to me about anything. I'm a good listener."

Laurie stiffened. "What did you hear?"

"Only what Will told me. That Cam didn't want to get married. Such a child. You need an older man. Someone who's ready to settle down."

"Or an older woman," Mal said casually, keeping those intense, piercing eyes on her.

She knew? How did she know? And how dare she out Laurie like this, in front of Vic?

"If you swing that way," Vic said, laughing. "This is San Francisco, after all." He turned to Laurie. "Well, if Mal's bowing out of the race, that just leaves you with better pickings, doesn't it?"

He thought *Mal* preferred women? Relief took the edge off Laurie's anger, but her skin still felt stretched thin, as if sizzling with static electricity.

Some of the men had returned, with glasses of champagne for them both and more drinks for themselves. Laurie was about to say something when a look on Mal's face stopped her. She turned to follow her gaze and saw the back of a photographer who was wandering around.

"Who's that?" Laurie asked.

"Press," Vic said, beaming. "I sent out a few invites. Techcrunch, Valleywag, Wired... nothing too big. Hang on, I'll bring him over here."

"No, wait—" she said, but he was gone. She turned to look at Mal, who seemed at an uncharacteristic loss, her posture loose and gaping, completely open to the room. Laurie had never seen her anything less than perfectly contained. It was unnerving. "Mal?"

She didn't seem to hear.

Vic came back, maneuvering to have one arm around Laurie and the other around Mal this time. Who didn't protest. Didn't even move. And the photographer's eyes fell on her and stayed there.

Oh. *Oh.*

Laurie's stomach lurched. If that was how Cam had looked at Will, how blind she'd been not to see it before! The camera flashed.

"Well, I suppose I'd better wander around," Mal said, and walked off before anyone else could speak.

"I'm Laurie," she said to the photographer.

"Kas." He shook her hand. His grip was graceful and strong. Thick, jet-black hair framed his fair face. He had deep laugh lines around his eyes, and when he smiled at her it was with a strange intensity, as if there was no one else in the room.

"Laurie, don't bother the man while he's working," Vic said, annoyed at being ignored.

"Of course," she said, and walked away to get some distance. To find Mal and ask her questions, so many questions.

Who is he? What happened between you two?

Mal was talking with someone about whether the iPhone, which had just come out that year, would change the Unicorn's strategy towards prioritizing mobile applications, her expression once again calm and focused, as if the last five minutes simply hadn't happened.

Maybe talking about technology pulled her together her the way focusing on other people's problems helped Laurie collect herself. Wondering about whatever had or hadn't happened between Mal and Kas certainly kept her mind off Sophia (who hadn't texted her). The work of tracking the invisible hurts and needs of others gave her a gyroscopic kind of stability—one that would wear off if she stopped moving.

"Who would've thought a college dropout could make the invention of the year?"

"On the contrary," Mal said, "it takes an innovative mind to veer off the beaten track. Someone who *can* drop out of college when everyone around them warns them it'll kill their career has exactly the kind of courage it takes to build something new."

The man she was speaking to scoffed. "Are you saying everyone here is inherently a sheep just because they stayed the course?"

"We're certainly more risk-averse," Mal said amicably. "We have student loans to repay."

"Jobs dropped out of *Reed*. They're not even in the top twenty. He was risking more by staying on, paying them for an education that wouldn't even get him in the door today."

Laurie swallowed down her nausea. What would they think of her if they knew that she cried with joy when she was accepted into Carleton, but couldn't afford to go? She'd only applied because they didn't charge an application fee.

"You're assuming everyone's goal is to join a tech company and climb the corporate ladder," said a deep voice behind her. Laurie turned to see Kas, the photographer. "What if all you wanted to do was write books, or travel the world, or raise a family?"

The men started laughing, as if he'd said something hilarious. Kas didn't react. His dark eyes fell on Mal, as if challenging her to a duel.

"You can't raise a family on a writer's salary," someone said, "but you can always write a book from your island home in Bali if you had a tech salary."

"Yes," Kas said, without looking away from Mal, "I suppose that's the logical thing to do."

Mal flinched at the word *logical*, as if it were a curse. She drew herself up. "I suppose you have to know what you want out of life," she said. "Be really *sure*."

In all the times Laurie had heard that word, she'd never made it sound like this. As if it contained venom. Mal tossed back the last of her champagne and held up the empty glass as her parting salvo.

Laurie went after her.

"You ready to go home?" Mal asked, with a smile that didn't reach her eyes.

"If you are."

They grabbed their coats and left, waving to Vic rather than prolonging their exit. They headed towards Mission Street to catch a cab, ignoring the catcalls from the homeless men along the way.

Laurie decided to play Mal's game, making assumptions for her to rebut or verify. "So why did you and Kas break up?"

Mal's lips twitched with amusement. "To break up, you'd have to have been a couple. We never were."

"Why not?"

"I suppose we both got cold feet. You never know if you truly want something until you have it within arm's reach." She flagged down a cab and got inside.

"I've only ever heard the opposite," Laurie said, following her in. "That you have to lose it to know."

Even breaking up with Cam hadn't hurt as much as turning down her college acceptance.

"We'd have had to fight our families to be together," Mal said. "He's a Pakistani, and a Muslim. He wanted kids, and I didn't. At least one of us would have had to give up on our more—" She rolled her eyes—"*artistic* ambitions, if we were to survive financially."

"So what he said, about writing books, traveling the world... those were *your* dreams?"

"A long time ago." She closed her eyes and leaned back.

Laurie's throat closed up. Why, when Mal had closed the door so firmly on her own dreams, did it hurt *her* as if she'd done the same? All this time, she'd thought Mal thrived in tech because she was *different*. To know they shared artistic ambitions only highlighted her own compromises.

She thought of the summer her family had spent camping in national parks, when four people living out of a car had grown untenable. At night, they'd set up tent and eat beans cooked on a stove fashioned out of Coke cans. While her brothers slept, she'd practice Bach on the keyboard piano that so desperately needed new batteries it sounded like a strangled cat.

"You have to wonder if it's a blessing or a curse," Mom said, "these so-called gifts we have. If you had to spend your life in a dark cave with only a slit through which you saw the stars, would you be grateful for that sliver of heaven? Or would you resent being offered a taste of something you could never have?"

It was the first time she'd said *we*, as if musical talent was a shared secret, an inheritance Laurie might grow into one day.

"Grateful," she said, immediately.

Mom sighed. But she taught Laurie first to read music, then to hear it. Every morning, her brothers drove the car into town to find a Home Depot or Lowe's to wait for work. People paid them to carry things, to install new toilet seats or curtain rods, or to put sod down in the lawn. Meanwhile, Laurie practiced on the keyboard, but also learned to hear the squirrels bounding inside of Paganini, to see Debussy as light scattered by the rain around her, and to feel the crystalline precision of Liszt in the summer sky.

"I wanted to be an artist," she said suddenly, as they made their way out of the taxi and Mal opened the front door. "I couldn't afford college, so I pretended to be a student so I could audit classes at Cornell."

She waited, pulse pounding, for the words she'd heard before. *So you cut in front of people who paid to come here? People who earned their place?*

But Mal only smiled. "Well, looks like we have another Steve Jobs right here."

"You don't think less of me?"

"Why should I?" Mal gave her a warm look. "You knew what you wanted and went after it the only way you could. That took guts."

Laurie stared at her, stupefied. Mal was supposed to remind her that her dreams were impossible, that she ought to shut them down as she had hers. Furious tears sprang to her eyes.

Mal's phone beeped with an incoming text message. She glanced at it, then showed it to Laurie. It was from Kas.

Nice to see you after all this time. Want to get coffee and catch up?

"Maybe I'll get a chance to do the same," Mal said.

chapter five

the housing market crashed in early 2008 and the Darling lost a third of its value. But there were still house parties, boat parties, and street parties in the Castro, fueled more now by grim resolve than exuberance.

"We've done this before," Vic assured investors, regaling war wounds from the first Dotcom bust. "This is just a small correction." As if the collecting masses on the street rightly belonged there.

Those who hadn't yet jumped onto Barack Obama's bandwagon of hope searched elsewhere for guides through the abyss, for yoga instructors and shamans, for a god or a growth mindset, for anyone who might offer them a shred of stability or help them climb a slightly higher hill of happiness.

After Will, Vic's new second-in-command only had to come in to work before noon to seem competent. His fatal mistake was doing more.

"Hustle is the name of the game," Raj announced at a team meeting. "Some of us have become too comfortable. Forgotten what it means to be hungry."

Laurie pictured him joining the ranks outside Boogaloos

with a sign. *Hungry. Will make presentations for a burger.*

He pushed Laurie as if she were a falcon he were coaching to flying weight. "You're smart, but you lack ambition. You fall apart under pressure. We need to change that." He accompanied his diagnosis with a prescription of self-help and management books. "In this new climate, you'll need to go beyond the specific job description. Anticipate what the project needs to succeed."

Raj took it on himself to diagnose the entire team. Then one day Laurie received a text that jolted her out of bed at 6 a.m.

I'm having trouble accessing the network. Can you contact Vic to fix it?

She should have gone back to bed, but the message was marked as read. Vic wouldn't be awake at this hour. She should have given him Vic's phone number and told him to sort it out.

Instead she knocked on Mal's door.

Mal's eyebrows danced a bit in amusement and confusion. She logged on in the dark, the screen lighting the planes of her face in cyber-chic.

"Good news, strange news," she said. "The network isn't down. But Vic's sent me a message asking if I can take over some of Raj's duties."

A chill passed through Laurie's chest. Their eyes met.

"He was good to you," Mal said. It was about as much of a question as she was capable of. Pausing for an objection.

What must it be like, to feel challenge and criticism as love? To not feel a flood of relief that scrutiny had passed by? Right now, Laurie simply stared at the text from Raj and contemplated replies.

The network isn't down. You've been fired.

I can't reach Vic. Here's his number. (Thank you and goodbye)

"Never outshine the master," Mal said. "It's the first law of power."

It was too early for this. "So you'll bite your tongue and keep your head down for *Vic*?"

"Don't you?"

Exposed. Projection was such a bitch.

They went into work to deal with the fallout.

"How long can you surf the wave without wiping out?" an engineer Laurie passed in the office kitchen asked his friend. "Whether it's a startup or a relationship, investment is about intuition. That's all you have to ride on."

Two days later he was laid off, and two months after that Mal and Laurie found him performing stand-up comedy at a club in the Tenderloin. Four years later he'd be driving a Lyft car with a pink mustache to supplement his freelance income. It was a warning to those who lived too large, and torture for those who'd stumbled but couldn't escape the orbit of the stars they'd sought.

Laurie stalked Sophia's Facebook page in a masochistic streak, and discovered she had moved in with two of her exes. She was taking one of them to rehab and helping the other one transition to becoming a woman. Sophia called herself the 'anchor of their polycule,' sending Laurie on a long research journey into metamours and vees, hinges and comets, all of which left her heartsick beyond endurance.

Then there was the photographer. Kasim Ashakzai. Any time Kas came by, Mal's face turned to him like a flower straining toward the sun. Laurie had to concede there was something magnetic about his Mona Lisa smile, about the depths of unfixable and unnameable unhappiness in his eyes. He walked tall, with an air of willful difference as dangerous as a dagger in the belt, all the while trailing a cologne that smelled like the pinecone air of untrammeled Himalayan peaks.

God, she wanted to paint him. He itched under her skin. But more than that she wanted to be rid of him, and of Mal, both of whom reminded her of her own loneliness. She could hear them laughing in the next room.

"Whatever happened to your Lollywood movie career?"

"Turns out the American who was funding my movie was actually a drug-smuggler," Kas said. "One day ISI busted into our set and took him away, and now it's an international incident."

"That's the trouble with our people, Kas," Mal said. "Romance can't be simple. It has to involve drug-smugglers. And global intrigue."

"We actually ran into glycerin shortages for the sad scenes. Oh, you didn't know? You get a tear-stick, although a Q-tip will do, dab it with glycerin, and—"

"That's... wait, what? Fake tears?" Mal sounded delighted.

"What did you think was happening? People stabbing themselves in the thigh off-camera? Real emotion? What did you think this was, Sundance?"

"Can I buy glycerin at Walgreens?"

"Who knows. I earned mine. Girls go wild for my tear-stick."

At Mal's peal of laughter, Laurie put in her earphones. These days, she had to hide her love for *It's a Wonderful Life* more than she needed to hide her erotica. Which Mal had found by accident when she returned too early from a business trip and handed over with, "City library books are *way* more interesting than suburban ones."

So when Laurie met Adam, who said *y'all* and called baristas *Ma'am* and told her how lonely he was in San Francisco, where women expected sex on the third date or sooner, but he couldn't *make love* to someone until he'd said and heard the *three little words*, she was smitten. He apologized for his balding head; she traced the edges of his widow's peak and regretted ever having fallen for Cam's young adult fantasy looks.

"I want something real," she said.

Three months into their relationship, Mal and Kas were off somewhere, edging towards something without ever getting there, while Adam came over to spend the day. He had to work, but wanted her company while he did. They were at separate ends of the couch, each on their laptop, when she got a message from Mal.

A picture of an extremely complicated menu of a coffee shop, tagged, *Remember when coffee was a beverage and not a geography quiz?*

She chuckled and typed up a response.

"What's so funny?"

She looked up. Adam was looking at her with a strange expression.

"It's Mal."

"What does she say?"

"Nothing important."

Adam picked at threads on the cushion. "I don't think she likes me very much."

"She doesn't like *anyone* very much."

"You're sure she isn't jealous?"

A graceless bark of a laugh escaped her. Mal? Jealous of him?

"It's not *that* strange," he said. "When two friends have been single for a long time, one can feel jealous when the other starts dating."

Oh, he meant Mal might be jealous of *her*.

"Mal doesn't want a relationship," she explained. "Where's all this coming from?"

He looked away. "I just don't think she's invested in your happiness."

"Why do you say that?"

"You deserve so much better. This is a rent-controlled apartment, isn't it? You've been generous enough to share it with her even though she makes enough to afford her own place, and she doesn't even acknowledge you. Does she really consider you a friend, or is she using you?"

Laurie pulled back, but he grabbed her hands and held them.

"I know so many people like her," he went on. "You and I, we'll never fit into their crowd. To them, we barely exist except as proof of their open-mindedness."

A pang went through her chest, even as she shook her head in protest. She understood, of course; her coworkers were polite enough not to talk about it in front of her, but she knew they spent their weekends at wineries and Michelin star restaurants. Mal wasn't like that. And they were friends, not just roommates.

Right?

Adam's eyes fell on the laptop, the shiny new MacBook he'd bought her. "I knew within two days of meeting you that you needed a new laptop, and you're telling me she *lives* with you and didn't notice you kept asking to borrow hers?"

Until he said it, she'd thought the opposite, that her friendship with Mal was so strong that she didn't even mind Laurie seeing her browser history.

That evening, Adam went back to his own place while Mal and Kas came by around eight. Laurie asked them about their day, hating that she was only doing it to see if Adam had a point, or if Mal would ask about her day too.

"Productive," Mal said. "We spent the entire day at Ritual, writing." She inclined her head. "Well, editing, mostly. I couldn't get anything new onto the page. Oh!" She dashed into her room and came back out with a torn envelope, handed it over to Kas. "Here's the rejection I was telling you about."

"Rejection?" Laurie asked.

"Kas convinced me I should send my story out to agents. One of them was kind enough to give me a reasoned rejection."

"*Reasoned*?" Kas asked, his beautiful dark eyes widening with wrath. "This is—I might not make it to the end of this. I'm your friend and I'm going to do my best, but you know this is not about you, right?"

Laurie tensed as Kas started pacing, holding the letter out in front of him to read. Mal leaned against the wall, entirely relaxed and amused. Laurie marveled at her calm for a moment, before she remembered—it was only to her, not Mal, that a man's anger meant upheaval. The narrow hallway between them seemed an uncrossable chasm.

Am I your token blue-collar friend?

"Did they really ask you to read Jane Eyre to understand romance better?" Kas asked. "It's like they're saying, why don't you go be a nice colonized child and read some white-people love so we can understand your story better?"

Mal grinned at Laurie, as if she'd understand, as if Mal had ever shown her any of her writing. She hadn't known about any of this.

"Your sentence structure is unusual," Kas went on, "so I'm guessing English isn't your first… wow. What century are we living in that anybody is allowed to assume that about anybody else? I'm trying to finish this but—" He groaned in despair. "Your story needs more eroticism. Meaning what, sex? God forbid that intimacy and love can look different for people from different cultures, or with different values."

"You're sweet," Mal said, laughing. She reached forward and plucked the letter out of his hands and gave it to Laurie. "Kas has always believed in my writing, even when the whole world stands against him."

"Well, the world needs correction," Kas said, folding his arms.

Shortly after, he left—so far, to Laurie's knowledge, he'd never spent the night—and Mal landed heavily on the couch.

"How was your day?" Mal asked, and even if she was flicking through the channels as she did, something in Laurie's chest loosened.

"Adam came by."

"Hm."

It could've just been a filler, a way to signal that she should move on. Or was it judgment?

"You don't like Adam?"

Mal shrugged. "I don't have an opinion about him either way."

"He's important to me."

Mal looked at her, confused. "Okay…"

"We might move in together," Laurie said, although it wasn't true. Not even close.

"Will you go to him, or do you need me to move out?"

"I—I don't know yet."

Why couldn't Mal show some modicum of emotion? Laurie's blood slowly pulsed up through her cheeks and then down to her throat where it seemed to clot with unsaid words. She wanted Mal to be unhappy at having to move out. To *react*, so Laurie would exist in equal measure.

"Sure, whatever you need," Mal said, with a smile that cracked her heart.

. . .

On one of the first warm weekends of the year, Adam was away on a business trip, so when Mal invited her to join her and Kas on a road trip to Marin, Laurie joined in so eagerly she forgot her iPhone at home. Most people didn't yet have smartphones, and she only had hers because Adam had bought it for her, so she counted her blessings she hadn't forgotten sunscreen and stopped worrying about it. It wasn't as if she was going to wander off on her own.

Mal drove (of course) taking Van Ness up to Lombard and then winding her way west towards the Golden Gate Bridge. Around them, the foghorns in San Francisco lowed the morning prayer like weird West Coast mullahs. The three of them argued about whether the bridge itself was vermilion or cadmium red or if they ought to accept that it was international orange just because the internet said so, while below them the boats of Sacramento hummed their tinny bubblegum sound. Once they got to Muir Woods, Laurie collected fallen acorns, remarking on the little x's on their heads, as if they had been marked out for greater purpose.

It was only as they headed further north to Point Reyes to lunch that she started to wonder why they'd asked her to come along. She kept quiet, not wanting to be a third wheel, but it seemed they both wanted her as a buffer between them. When she came up close, she heard them arguing.

"How long can you keep trying to get the permission to live the life you actually want to live?" Mal was saying, a thread of unmistakable bitterness in her voice. "If you want to write, write."

"It's easy for you to say. You can take it or leave it, you have alternatives. A whole lucrative career you can fall back on as a consolation prize."

"I *knew* my job bothered you."

Laurie fell back, out of hearing distance. This was the most emotion she'd heard from Mal, and even now she was restrained. Everything about her was. Although she wore a summer dress, a firm belt tempered flighty folds. Her long legs were weighed down by heavy hiking boots. Lines triumphed over curves, deliberation over whimsy.

As they drove back to San Francisco, along the curves of Highway 1, the waves to their right were ten feet high and crashed against the cliffs louder than thunder. From time to time Mal cast a look at Kas that was ravenous with desire, but he looked ahead serenely, as if he wasn't between two oceans, one on each side, each of them dark and devouring.

They dropped Kas off, then left the Zipcar in its stall and walked home. Laurie found her phone still connected to its charger, beeping urgently.

Seven missed calls from Adam.

She called him back immediately, heart pounding.

"Where have you been? I've been mad with worry."

"I was out with Mal. What's wrong?"

"The vet called. Perry needs chemo. The surgery wasn't enough. I—I can't think. Should I get a second opinion? Why didn't he tell me before the surgery that chemo might still be necessary?"

"Breathe, darling. We researched this, remember? Chemo is less aggressive for cats than it is for humans."

"I don't know if I want to put Perry through this. My dad had chemo. It changed him, and he died anyway. In pain and miserable. Am I overthinking this? You don't think I'm being cheap, do you? It's about the pain, not the money."

"Whatever you choose, I'll support you. When do you get back? Will you need me to come over to help? Should I cancel the Tahoe trip?"

They were supposed to go away together next weekend, with a couple of his friends.

There was a moment of silence, and then Adam swore under his breath.

"I completely forgot about the Tahoe trip. Perry's going to be vomiting. I can't leave him alone."

"Don't worry about it," Laurie said, mildly relieved. Adam had paid for all of it, and it was ridiculously expensive. "I'll call the lodge and cancel."

"We can't," Adam said. "The room was booked with a non-refundable group rate, because Miguel and Shawna are going too. It's all such a goddamn waste."

Laurie didn't particularly love Perry, who was cantankerous even when he wasn't projectile-vomiting, but he was a *cat*. A poor, sick cat.

Sunk cost, she remembered Mal saying, so many months ago, in a taqueria bathroom.

"What do you want to do, love?" she asked.

"I don't know. It's all so unfair."

"Do you have other friends who might be willing to take our room? When I'm feeling down, it always makes me feel better to make someone else happy."

"You're a sweetheart. But I'm too upset to think right now. Why weren't you answering your phone?"

"I told you. I left it at home when I went out with Mal."

"It wasn't on the calendar," he said, and his tone was different now.

Oh, right. The calendar. He'd shown her how to use it on the laptop, so they could coordinate logistics more easily. They'd snuggled for an hour booking the Tahoe trip details together. But she hadn't thought of using it for her own personal needs, and the road trip had been spontaneous…

"Laurie?"

"You know how I am with technology, love. I don't use it unless I have to. The screens give me a headache."

His tone grew tight with pain. "Laurie, we've talked about this. You know what it does to me when I don't know where you are. Where my mind goes. You can't seriously be doing this to me right now when I'm already going through so much shit."

Suddenly shifting into auto-pilot, she responded in the gentlest and most apologetic of tones. "You're right, of course. I'm sorry."

"This isn't about me, Laurie. You have to remember to take your phone with you. What if you got lost? Your phone is your lifeline."

"Of course, Adam. I understand."

• • •

Laurie washed the dishes. She held the phone to her ear by tipping her head sideways almost into her neck. Mom was going on about the regatta at the Geneva summer festival, and she debated an appropriate way to ask, *Mom, remember when I was five and we ran away from home? When did Dad first start scaring you?*

As if attuned to her thoughts, Mom said, "I didn't raise you right, Lo. You're too independent, and you don't need a man. It's so tough seeing other people's kids get married, knowing my Lo's all alone."

"Mom, I'm fine."

"Just because I couldn't make it work, you shouldn't think—"

"I don't."

There was a disbelieving sniffle at the other end of the line.

Laurie sighed. "Whatever Dad did to you—"

"Not to me, Lo. Never to me. He came back from the war broken, and what was I going to do, turn him away?"

"Then... why did we leave?"

"He broke Micah's arm—by accident! Your brother just caught him in the middle of an episode, and the PTSD... Anyway, I drove Micah to the hospital. I don't think your father knew until then that I could drive. I'd always been letting him do it. After that, he was different."

"But what finally made you decide to leave? I mean, you can barely hang up on telemarketers."

Mom didn't answer for a long time. Laurie was just about to change the subject when she said, "You know, honey, I don't remember that day at all. I didn't plan it or anything. Sometimes I think I'd always been planning to leave, and one day while my mind was asleep my body just woke up and drove away."

. . .

By the autumn of 2008, almost everyone who still had a job had a therapist too, and some, like Adam, kept a copy of the DSM-5 on their coffee table to help any visiting guests determine whether what they really needed to be happy was medication or a move to another state. Laurie kept her head down at work and tried not to pay attention to the rumors that the Unicorn might not survive the year.

"Everyone's moving to Seattle these days, buying the dip."

"Mark's been living in his Prius, did you know?"

"Well, he did spend three months on a waitlist for that car."

Adam worked eighty or even ninety-hour weeks, and even Mal grew quiet, thoughtful, although that might have been because Kas was around less too. Laurie saw on Facebook that he was traveling, and articles he'd written told her he was in L.A., in Denver, in New York and Portland.

Vic got divorced and went to Burning Man, and came back with the conviction he could commune with the dead. Nick left the company to join the Obama campaign, and Laurie finally found the strength to stop following Sophia's Facebook feed. It felt as if they were all holding their breath, in suspended animation, unflinching in their belief that all it would take to turn the economy and their lives around was the election of one man from Illinois to the presidency.

One night in October, Mal knocked on her door. "Hey, Laurie, I—I've misplaced my laptop. May I use yours to buy a new one?"

Laurie startled out of bed, wondering how she was so calm. "Of course! But how? Are you all right?"

Mal gave her a tired smile that didn't reach her eyes, and held her hands out for the laptop. "I'm fine."

"You're sure?"

She opened a new browser window. "I'm sure. I just need to—Laurie, what's this?"

Mal brought the cursor to the top of the screen where a small red ticker was flashing.

"That's Adam's calendar application. Whenever it flashes red I need to authorize it."

Laurie clicked on the ticker and pressed the OK button on the dialog that appeared.

A complicated suite of emotions crossed Mal's face.

"Is everything okay?"

"Yes, thank you." Mal closed the laptop and held her wrist. Her fingers were ice-cold and trembling. She pulled her out into the hallway without saying a word.

"Mal? It's cold out here. And I'm in my PJ's."

"Laurie, that's not a calendar application."

Her blood turned to ice. "Then what is it?" But she already knew.

"It's a screen recorder and camera, so he can see your face and anything that's on your screen whenever he wants to."

Laurie was no longer cold. She was simply numb, floating outside her body. But the admin in her was processing information faster. "We need to change the locks. Adam has a key."

"You can't use your phone," Mal said. "If there's a matching app, there's probably a tracker on that too."

Mal sprang the $200 for a locksmith to come overnight, and the two of them huddled together in the living room while he worked, communicating silently with paper and pen like children at a campfire. Mal searched every crevice for cameras and bugs while Laurie shivered and muttered, "He was probably too cheap for any real spyware."

She had half a mind to call her brother Jack, who had once driven her to Walgreens in the middle of the night to buy tampons, but had also smashed her piano so she couldn't be disappointed wanting things she couldn't have. It was right around when his ex moved to the city and he spent a week's paycheck at the Army Surplus store on materials to climb into a high-rise building.

You aren't seriously going to stalk her, Jack!

I'm just worried about her, alone in New York. She's not very street smart. I just want to teach her to be prepared.

The sky outside the window grew lighter, became a steely gray. Mal called in to work and said they'd both come down with a highly contagious cold. Adam's call came around 8 AM.

"Hey, love," Laurie said to Adam out of habit, and then winced.

Mal spat her coffee.

"Hey, you up for getting coffee at Ritual before I have to get to work?"

"But your office is in SoMa," Laurie said. "We can just get dinner later."

Mal retreated to her room, a bagel lodged in her mouth and disapproval in her eyes.

"I don't mind," Adam said. "I woke up missing you. I had the strangest dream."

"Oh?"

"Yeah, anyway, it would really help to see you. To hold you."

"What kind of dream was it?"

"You'll laugh."

"Have I ever?"

"Melissa did, all the time," Adam said.

Laurie sank into the couch. It was going to be that kind of

conversation then. How had she not realized Adam bored her?

"I hurt you, didn't I, bringing up Melissa?" he asked.

She went quiet, waiting for him to tantrum himself out.

"You have no idea what you do to me," he said. "The power you have."

Oh, this is how he keeps you in his orbit. He makes you feel that you're the one pulling the strings.

"It was just a dream," Adam said. "I know you wouldn't hurt me. Especially when Perry's dying and you know my project's due at the end of the month."

"What did I do in this dream?" she asked.

"You know I love you, right?" Adam said.

"Of course."

Adam waited, as if expecting an I-love-you-too, and then said, "And I've told you all my secrets. I've only ever been with one other woman."

"Did you want to know my past lovers?" she asked. This conversation was strange, surreal.

"I don't need to," Adam said. "As long as they're in the past."

"I've had a few, but only three that counted. Two men, and one woman."

She'd admitted it voluntarily because the thought of the alternative was exhausting. He'd poke around for a while, mention that he dreamed of her leaving him, talk about the absurdity of it, demand to be reassured—better to rip the Band-aid off as fast as possible.

"Was it the girl from your Facebook photos? The one with the red hair?"

"Adam, there's no girl with red hair in my Facebook photos." And there wasn't. All photos with Sophia had been deleted or untagged, so the only way he could know of their existence was if he had recorded her screen when she'd visited Sophia's profile in moments of weakness.

From there the conversation devolved. In fifteen minutes, Adam managed to scold her for ruining his mood right before an exec meeting, accuse her of leading him on and of sleeping with him for money.

When she hung up, Laurie had a headache.

At least it's over.

Except the thing about relationships in San Francisco was that because they were so poorly defined, so unconventional, they were often impossible to end. How, after all, could you kill something that had never really been alive?

Two hours later Laurie received a spreadsheet in her email in which Adam had carefully documented her failings as well as how much money he had spent during their relationship.

June 7, 2008: Responded to 300-word affectionate email with 1 sentence + emojis.

July 1, 2008: Bailed on Gary Danko reservation because of PMS. Reservation not refunded.

Her head spun. She revisited each of these moments, trying to remember whether there was any truth to the accusations. She wasn't one for long emails; she'd never learned the right way to type, and two fingers stabbing at cold and cranky buttons had never been her love language. How quickly Adam had typed this all up! If she were more tech savvy, she'd know how to look at the version history on the file, to see how long he'd been keeping score.

Eventually Mal came out of her room. "We should get you a new laptop too," she said. "No sense holding on to that thing."

Laurie showed Mal Adam's email without a word, waited for her outrage and fury to help her access her own. But it never came. Mal glanced at the spreadsheet with confusion. Her nostrils flared. Then she chuckled and tossed the laptop aside.

"Come," Mal said, leaping off the sofa and offering her a hand. "Let's go to the Apple store and pick something out. Then we won't have to wait for shipping."

"But—" It felt so strange to leave an email unreplied, like walking out of the house without turning off the stove.

Mal was already wearing her shoes. Laurie had never got used to it, how Mal's healthy disregard for the impossible, when it came to work projects, transitioned smoothly to an unhealthy disdain for the inconvenient in daily life. There was no emotion she couldn't suppress when it suited her.

Maybe hers was the better way. After all, what had Laurie's approach gotten her? She got up and followed Mal, as if in a dream. Within two hours they were already returning home laden with large bags.

Adam was waiting for them, pacing outside the building. When he saw Mal, his face clouded over and he came to a standstill.

"I've been trying to reach you all day," he said to Laurie. "I couldn't just leave things the way they were, so I came over on my lunch break."

If he'd tried entering, he made no mention of the fact that his keys didn't work.

Mal placed her bag down and leaned against the metal railing, signaling that she wasn't going to leave.

"Do you mind—?" Adam asked her with a glare.

Mal blinked innocently. "Mind what?"

"This is a private conversation," he said, drawing himself up to his full height to tower over her. Laurie could have told him how useless it would be, how often people at work tried to intimidate Mal without success.

"Oh, I'm not familiar with the concept," Mal said coolly. "Privacy must be a guy thing, they so rarely let us have it."

He must have sensed he wasn't getting anywhere with her, because he turned to Laurie. "You have to forgive me. This morning—I don't know what came over me. I was out of my mind. Between Perry and work, I was stressed… but you have to know how you came across. The things you said—I had no idea you were capable of such cruelty."

There was no explaining the gravitational pull of a narcissist to someone who hasn't felt it. He had hooks into her softest, most vulnerable parts, and he pulled on them with the kind of skill he'd never shown in conversation or in bed.

"Real love looks past our worst selves," Adam said, more gently now. "This morning, we saw the worst of each other, but I'm still here, loving you. I forgive you, Laurie. I know you just pushed me away because you got scared, but I also know that in your heart of hearts you don't want to be alone."

The tears in his eyes drew tears to hers. She was shaking apart right there on the pavement, dissociating from the body that was standing with a laptop on Guerrero Street.

"But she's not alone," Mal said.

Laurie looked at her in confusion. Mal shrugged, as if she was only pointing out an obvious fact.

"You stay out of it," Adam said. "Haven't you done enough, poisoning her mind against me? The last thing she needs is advice from a slut who cares about no one but herself."

The word—*slut*—stung her like a slap. Short, sharp and vicious. Somehow, nothing Adam had said about her hurt the way his attack on Mal did.

"Mal, let's go home," she said.

"Laurie, this isn't like you," Adam said sternly. "I'm still processing what Melissa did to me, and the way you're acting... it's just very triggering."

She started shaking, unable to think. If not answering an email felt like her house would burn down, not apologizing when people confronted her felt like that entire burning house falling on her head.

A loud peal of laughter to her right snapped her out of it.

"You know," Mal said, still lounging against the railing nonchalantly, "if you installed spyware on this *Melissa's* laptop too, it's no wonder she left you."

His eyes widened in realization, and then fell to their hands, to the large white bags with the Apple logo. He glared at Laurie, and it took everything she had not to flinch or piss herself.

"I was going to just throw away the laptop you gave me," she said, "but if you stay here I'll—I'll take it to the police and bring up charges to get a restraining order."

That seemed to shock him into moving. He hissed, but walked past them towards Mission Street. Laurie climbed the first step up towards their house and promptly fell down.

"Take your time," Mal said, and sat down beside her on the stair.

There was so much she wanted to say—*thank you, how did you know? I'm sorry*—

"Would you like me to carry you in?"

Laurie shook her head. "Could you... hold me for a minute?"

Mal's arm came around her shoulders and pulled her close. Hugged her until she stopped shaking. Eventually, they carried the bags into the house. Quietly, moving in synchronicity, Laurie made lunch while Mal set up both laptops.

Later, after they'd both retreated into their rooms, she blocked Adam online. With his posts gone from her Facebook feed, a post from Kas from yesterday came into view. He was standing by a boat in Central Park, with his arm around a woman's waist. She held out a hand to the camera to show off a diamond ring.

Laurie read the caption nearly a hundred times without comprehending it. She finally leapt out of the bed and ran to Mal's room.

"What is it?"

"Mal—I just saw—have you seen? Kas…"

A mask came over her features. "Yes, I saw it yesterday."

"Are you all right?"

"I sensed it coming," she said with a smile. "I think, of the two of us, you've had the harder twenty-four hours. You should get some rest."

For a second Laurie almost believed her and walked away; then she remembered how much of a relief it was when your world was falling apart to help someone else put theirs back together. Somehow fate had conspired to let them have this together, as if they were running a three-legged race.

"I know how you felt about him, and—he loved you too."

"It's not that simple. I'm fine now, really."

"Meaning you weren't before?"

Mal chewed her lip, as if debating whether to say anything. Eventually, her shoulders sagged. "So, yesterday I left work early to get a coffee and waffle at Bluebottle. I wanted to sit by the Bay Bridge and write. That's when I saw it. I didn't take it well."

"What happened?"

"Remember how I told you I'd misplaced my laptop? I—um, threw it into the Bay."

Laurie's jaw dropped. They stared at each other, and then, in the same instant, burst into hysterical laughter.

chapter six

On the 4th of November, 2008, Mal joined the neighbors as they poured into the streets to celebrate Barack Obama's victory. Laurie hid in her room and cried. Prop 8 had passed in California, declaring the only valid marriage between a man and a woman. She hadn't even known she'd held out hope for a different kind of life.

Still, the election brought with it a heart-seizing, infectious joy that felt as precarious as driving along Highway 1, which she and Mal did every weekend.

"Do you have your travel bag?" Mal asked, as if she wasn't the one who always forgot something.

"Since you made us brush our teeth out with *body wash* I've always kept one ready."

If heartbreak made Laurie mope by the television with a bowl of candy, it made Mal restless and insatiable. They drove down to Big Sur blasting Blue Öyster Cult, singing along—*Home on the highway, Home isn't my way, Home I'll never be*—in rented Zipcars that they always brought back smelling of the ocean.

"I want to get *warm*," Mal said, driving them to Esalen, where she argued about the nature of the universe and theory of mind with naked hippies in stinking, sulfurous hot springs under a starry sky. But each time they got home, San Francisco's bone-chilling fog enveloped them like a specter, and they climbed the creaking stairs with heavy, leaden feet.

In no time, the year ended. The inauguration they'd waited for arrived, but January felt like an ending rather than a beginning, as if the party was over and it was now time to get to work. The stock and housing market had crashed, and in 2009 the adrenaline was jittering out of the collective American system, and everyone had to pick up the shattered pieces of their lives. Laurie's eldest brother Micah was in jail again, Jack's house was in foreclosure, and her mother was hunting for a new husband at the age of fifty-two.

"You never come home," said a sister-in-law who'd forgotten her existence for three years.

"Laurie's too good for us," Jack said in the background. "She couldn't wait to leave."

He wasn't wrong. The summer they'd all lived together, in a dilapidated house on the outskirts of Lansing, her mother taught her how to hide the markers of her upbringing—*nuclear, not nucular, Could you, not wouldja*—and how to dye the Ralph Lauren dresses they got from the thrift store to hide the stains.

"Worn luxury is better than new trash," her mother said, turning her nose up at T.J. Maxx. "People think poverty is contagious. Worse, the standards you accept in your clothes are the standards you accept in men."

Meanwhile, Jack came home holding a dead possum in one hand and a baseball bat in the other.

"Found this guy near the chicken coop," he said proudly. "Smashed 'is head in."

She and Jack both worked at Cornell University's Robert Purcell diner. Jack did the dishes, emptying trays of wasted food into Oscar, the large compost incinerator. Laurie's nails started to fray after three weeks of sorting wet silverware.

"You should wear gel nail polish," said Ian, the guy who shared her shift. "Shellac is, like, the only thing in the world that can handle the dish room."

Ian was a student, not a townie, but poor, and so he worked at the diner to pay back student loans. He was the first openly gay person she'd known, and his bright fuchsia nails were a welcome touch of beauty amidst all the slop and grease. Eventually the burly dish room staff stopped giving him shit about wearing eyeliner and Laurie stopped holding her breath waiting for something terrible to happen. Even Jack grudgingly started to respect Ian when he crawled underneath the stalled dish belt to restart it.

One night, Ian pulled away the last of the chocolate pie when it failed to maintain temp and got yelled at by a lacrosse player for being a Nazi. Then it was Jack who scared off the lacrosse player and comforted Ian. And on November 7, 2000, Laurie stumbled behind Jack in her frayed denim jeans that smelled of stale eggs, watching the students glued to CNN on the hanging television, and Ian came up and threw an arm around both their shoulders and said, "Fuck 'em all. As if either Bush or Gore has ever washed their own dishes, am I right?"

Jack grunted, and they went outside for a break.

"They're all crooks," Jack conceded. "Out for themselves."

"I mean, so am I," Ian said. "That's why I'm not going to stick around here. As soon as I graduate, I'm headed to San Francisco."

"Are they all like you out there?" Jack asked.

"God, I hope so," Ian said, laughing.

Laurie was already lost to her family then, although Jack wouldn't know it for a while. Ian had given her something she hadn't imagined possible, a future filled with pretty men who wouldn't hurt her and nail polish that wouldn't betray her, both waiting across the country, in San Francisco. Someday.

And in March 2009, just when she'd finally given into the allure of Barack Obama, had started once more to feel the hope that she'd suffocated for eight years, she was laid off.

• • •

Of course Mal knew, but Laurie didn't want to talk about it, so Mal simply brought home a tub of Bi-Rite's salted caramel ice-cream and let her wallow by the TV. Laurie wondered what it would take for Mal to offer the kind of affection she'd come to expect from growing up on family-friendly TV shows—what would merit a hug? Then again, who knew if Mal had grown up on the same shows, or if she'd watched them in stupefaction wondering at the human species. Some of the treats Mal brought home reminded her of a cat bringing home dead birds.

During the day, when Mal was away, Laurie got hooked on *Breaking Bad*; all her frustrations found voice in Walt White's desperate bid for transformation.

Those days, under the billboards that spoke of cloud computing and middleware, brawls broke out in dive bars and empty auto-shops. Lifetimes were spent on the highways leading to Silicon Valley, on 280 and 85 and 101, and the worn grooves in the carpool lane were the only kind of graffiti anyone had time to make anymore. So, yeah: Walt White was everyone.

She found work waitressing, but couldn't get enough hours to qualify for health insurance. One day, she was heading out just as Dolores came in to clean, and it was just as embarrassing as getting in that Lyft to be driven around by her former coworker, only the other way around. She couldn't get out fast enough.

That weekend, in an attempt at making peace with her family, Mal invited her mother, sister and brother over for dinner. They'd talked on the phone a bit over the last year, but this was the first time they'd see each other in person since Mal's break with them in Tahoe.

"Are you sure you want me around?" Laurie asked. "If it's a family thing, I could wait in Ritual until you're done."

"You're not leaving me alone with them. Besides, if you're here, there's a chance they'll behave. Or at least leave early."

Mal took them around the city in the afternoon, and then brought them over around six. Two women and one man appeared with her, all of them clearly surprised to see Laurie on the landing.

"I'm Mal's roommate."

"Hi," said one of the women. "I'm Aditi."

Mal's sister was shorter than her, petite and dainty where Mal was tall and muscular. Her brother, Ashwin, was gray-haired and balding at thirty-five, and their mother was tall and thin, with deep lines of worry and sadness etched into her skin.

They sat down to dinner and Mal's mother asked, "So what is it you do, Laurie?"

Panic bubbled up in her chest, and Mal shot her a look of concern.

"There's no need to interview her, Mom."

"I was asking a simple question. Being polite."

"I'm a waitress," Laurie said.

Confusion clouded Mal's mother's face, while her sister and brother exchanged glances Laurie thought were laden with disappointment. Mal had warned her about this, how they looked down on her for only having a Bachelor's degree and never bothering to get her MBA.

"So you're still in school then?"

"Mom!"

"I'm just asking, what it is she plans to *do*? For her career, I mean."

"Laurie's an artist," Mal said, "and a musician."

Something about that silenced the group, as if she'd just announced that Laurie was an emu rather than a person.

Mal brought out the dinner she'd cooked.

"I'm impressed you still have time to cook," Aditi said. "If it wasn't for our maid, I'd starve."

"Well, she doesn't have to take care of kids, as we do," Ashwin said. "And most of tech is cushy compared to banking."

"Poor Ashwin had to sleep in the office many nights," Mal's mother said to Laurie. "For the first ten years of his job, we never saw him. They squeeze every last drop out of you."

"It's an investment. You work hard for ten years, and you're set for the rest of your life," Ashwin said. He curled his fingers daintily around the rice in his plate, little finger rising apart. "But of course, if you can't discipline yourself now, you'll be working into your seventies because you won't have enough put away to buy a house, never mind retire."

"At least I'll go into my seventies with all my hair," Mal said, glaring.

"Where did you go to school, Laurie?" Aditi asked.

So, it would be frying pan to fire.

"Grayson Academy," she said, thinking they weren't likely

to know it was a high school.

"I don't know that one," Mal's mother said.

"Must be an art school," Aditi said.

Dinner went on with no further dangers for her, although the barbs came fast and sharp for Mal. Did Laurie know she'd been accepted to Stanford where she could have stayed at home, but *chose* to go all the way east to Cornell, disappointing everyone? If only Mal had gone into finance, she'd have a house by now, like all the others in her class. How lonely Mal must be in San Francisco, without children to pass the time.

After dinner, Laurie excused herself to her room, but couldn't concentrate on her painting, not when she could hear them arguing in the living room.

"I no longer pray that you get married," Mal's mother said. "I pray that you're happy. We just want to understand."

"Understand what?"

"Just *talk* to us openly and let us know what's going on with you," Ashwin said, "otherwise we can't solve this problem."

"Which problem?"

Laurie marveled at how Mal's tone never rose up in anger, but remained calm even as her questions slowly dismantled her family's delusions. She had to smile. In the early days, she'd worried for Mal at work, when she asked seemingly stupid questions with perfect sincerity. But after the fourth time she brought a pointless meeting to an abrupt, productive end by revealing some false assumption or questioning some hyperbolic claim, Mal became known as the velvet knife—her patient, persistent questions always cut through to the heart of things.

"Mal, this is no life," Aditi said, sounding impatient. "You're not a child, to be living with *roommates*. At this rate, you'll be forty-five and alone, with nothing to show for yourself but a couple of cats."

"Is that a problem? If I find someone that makes me happy I won't push them away. But I don't care to be married, and I don't want kids."

"Your grandmother would die of shock. The only reason she's still holding on at ninety-one is to see your kids," said her mother.

Laurie hugged her chest hard, feeling as if someone had kicked her in the ribs.

"Yeah, that's no pressure at all," Mal said. "Look, this isn't a conversation I'm interested in having. Can we talk about something else?"

"How can we?" Ashwin asked. "This is your *future*!"

"It's also my *present*," Mal said. "You've been planning this conversation all day. When we were on the Golden Gate Bridge, your mind wasn't there. You couldn't enjoy it. You couldn't watch the sunset. All you wanted to do was get it over with so we could have this—this intervention."

"You can't stay distracted from everything that matters in life with *fun*," Ashwin said, spitting out the last word.

Even through the door, his tone felt hot to the touch.

Mal only chuckled.

"There's little else that matters," she said. Then, her voice suddenly became icy, dangerous in the way that left grown men stuttering in her wake at work. "I'm not the container for other people's regrets or ambitions."

Later, after they left, Laurie was still tense, waiting for an explosion that hadn't happened. Mal knocked on her door.

"I take it you heard all that."

"Thin walls."

"Are you okay?"

"Me? Mal, that was..."

She shrugged. "Want to watch some TV?"

"Vampire Diaries?"

Mal sighed. "Hot people don't make up for bad writing."

"This is why your writing career is stuck," Laurie said, gathering her blanket. "You're trying to be sincere and literary, when really all anyone wants you to do is write about hot people being stupid."

For a second Mal didn't answer. Laurie whirled around to face her, afraid that she'd hurt her, afraid that after this evening's attacks she wouldn't have known she was joking.

To her surprise Mal was laughing so hard she made no sound, bent over double and clutching her stomach.

It made her own gut somersault with joy.

Oh, she was in *trouble*.

. . .

Mal's family might have intended to make her rethink her choices, but they only succeeded in making Laurie question hers. The friends she made waitressing all had the same story to tell—they were taking whatever jobs they could to make the rent, but any talk of savings would either start political arguments or drunken commiseration. Laurie didn't have energy for the former or money for the latter, so she kept quiet, paying her share of the rent without letting on that she had to dive into her reserves for groceries.

Although Mal offered, Laurie wasn't going to let her pay, not when she was spinning out of control. Mal might not have cried over that terrible dinner, and she never complained about the endless calls from her mother (who did cry, and loudly, all the time), but she went out dancing three nights a week and came home with bleeding feet, too drunk to notice the stains she left on the stairs. She signed up for Krav Maga, for parkour, for a course in urban escape and evasion that left taser burns on her arms.

In November, Mal went away to San Diego for a week, as did most senior execs at the Unicorn, for a leadership training seminar. When she came back, she sat on the couch for hours, seeing and saying nothing, until Laurie started to worry.

"It's nothing," Mal said when asked, then hesitated. "Actually, would you mind taking a look at something?"

She showed her a recording she'd made, surreptitiously, with her phone. A clean-cut man in his forties appeared in front of a large conference room, standing beside Vic, who looked at him with giddy adoration.

Laurie swallowed down the wave of fury at seeing Vic—after everything she'd done for him, he'd laid her off via a form email and deactivated her badge so he wouldn't have to face her.

"That's Keith, someone Vic hired to—" Mal made air-quotes—"lead the team to greater value and throughput, through self-awareness and accountability."

"What's that supposed to mean?"

"As far as I can tell, it involves recognizing my deep-set need to rebel against authority as a 'shifter strategy' about which I need to be honest with my assigned coach in our daily phone call."

Laurie sat down heavily. "Mal, that's a cult."

Mal smiled. "Yes, it is. I knew as soon as they made us promise not to talk to anyone about what we learned in the session. And then—" She continued the video.

The man, Keith, wore a suit over a simple white t-shirt, and projected an air of calm, easy authority. "You're all highly successful, type A people who've made it here by employing certain strategies. I'm here to tell you those won't get you any further. We're here to break you down and build you back up, more authentic and whole. Maybe you were bullied. Maybe your parents and friends don't really understand the work you do. How hard it is. How important. Your wounds hold you back, make you compete with each other to prove yourself. But here—here you've already arrived. You've already won, and the earth is yours to inherit."

Mal turned off the video. "You know when they said *The meek shall inherit the earth*, I hardly thought they were talking about inheriting all the drama that comes with having a bunch of fiber optic cables run beneath the sea."

"Mal..."

"I know."

"What are you going to do?"

"I ought to quit, but—"

But then nobody would be able to pay the rent. It hadn't occurred to her that Mal could be as trapped as she was.

She screwed up her courage to ask Mal the question that had been on her mind for months. "Why do you never talk to me about your writing?"

"Because you don't want me to."

"Why would you think that?"

"You get this look on your face, like when I showed you the rejection letter."

Laurie took a breath. "I was being petty. I thought we were... *close*, but that was something you'd shared with Kas, and never with me."

"Oh." Mal's face went through a series of emotions, from

confusion to guilt to something else Laurie couldn't quite place. She'd never heard her apologize for anything, but she got the sense from the way Mal's fingers twitched on the sofa that she wanted to.

"I thought—" Laurie inhaled deeply. If she didn't get it out now, it would fester. "I thought you didn't think I'd understand because I didn't… I'm not…"

"You're an idiot," Mal said, rolling her eyes. "You gave me a full whiteboard diagram of our system architecture to onboard me onto the team when even the tech lead couldn't—why would I ever doubt your intelligence?"

From anyone else she'd have called it last-minute flattery. She relaxed beside Mal, their fingers close enough to share warmth but not touching.

"Kas and I met in a writing class," Mal said, drawing her knees up to her chest. "I think, maybe, I liked the idea of us more than the reality. Two writers, breaking past the borders imposed upon us, determined to write about something other than mangoes or arranged marriage. I wanted us to collaborate on a novel. Two intertwined perspectives, achieving synthesis."

Laurie frowned. It sounded beautiful, but not… romantic. "He didn't want to?"

"No," Mal said, scratching absently at the fluff on the sofa. "I suppose I understand. Every writer wants to leave their own mark on the world. I don't blame him."

"I thought you were in love with him."

"I was," Mal said easily, oblivious to the audible crack in Laurie's heart. "Just not in the ordinary way. I don't feel things the same way as other people. But the way he writes, it whittles my insides. Leaves me feeling less…"

"Untranslatable?" Laurie asked, remembering her own

language from Tahoe.

"Yes," Mal said. "I don't want the same things as other people. I could care less about a husband or a house. I don't know how to explain it, but I loved him without wanting the ordinary things from him. He wanted all of them from me, though, and I couldn't stand it."

"So you couldn't be in a relationship with him and still write?" Laurie asked. Mal peered at her, as if she'd somehow said something very strange. It unnerved her, and she felt the need to ramble on. "I just mean, when we go on our weekend trips, you're able to write, so maybe you and he could have worked something out?"

"Huh," Mal said, as if something had just clicked into place. She stretched out and her foot started twirling again, a sure sign wheels were turning in her head.

"What is it?"

Mal smiled, a lopsided downward smile that made Laurie ache with its beauty. "Nothing. I just realized... if I felt *him* to be an intrusion, I could never have kids."

"I don't want kids either," Laurie confessed. "I've spent so much of my life struggling to take care of myself, I couldn't really take care of anyone else. And so many men want me to be their mother."

"So no more narcissistic parasites?" Mal asked, raising an eyebrow.

Laurie started laughing. "Speaking of parasites," she said, and turned on Vampire Diaries.

chapter seven

Laurie was in the middle of her shift waitressing at Caliente, when her coworker Ariel stepped up beside her and said, "I'm going to walk right behind you, okay? You're bleeding."

Her hands shook on the tray, but she held it and her smile steady and walked back to the kitchen to drop it off. Ariel followed her right up to the bathroom and waited outside.

"Kitchen apron, please?" Laurie said, staring at the blood on her jeans in surprise.

She fastened the black apron around her waist and tried not to think about it until the end of her shift. She'd just switched to a new birth control regimen and a little out-of-schedule spotting was to be expected.

It got worse. A week later, she was too dizzy to finish the shift, and had to run down to Walgreens for a Midol and a heavy pad.

"I'm saving up to get myself one of those," Ariel said, glancing at her groin, "but you're not marketing it very well."

"Maybe yours will come with a warranty," Laurie said weakly, to hide her worry. She couldn't afford to take a day off work to see a doctor.

"Are we out of sync?" Mal asked one day, coming out of the bathroom.

Her directness made Laurie wince. She'd tried so hard to bury the pad in the trash with wads of toilet paper, but the smell was strong.

"Yes, I'm on a new pill," she said.

Mal went into her room.

With a rush of pain came anger too, that Mal hadn't pressed further. They were out of sync in other ways too.

Recently, Mal had been... vacant. It was probably something she herself hadn't noticed, and her cold, unbroken efficiency made Laurie wonder if she was losing her mind.

A few weeks later, she caught Mal standing in the kitchen with an empty wine-glass in her hand and a lost look in her eyes.

"Mal?"

"Sorry, I spaced out. I wanted—" She stood on her tiptoes to reach with her fingertips for the wine bottle she kept in the rack on the top shelf. It was a beautiful, graceful movement, but it also lifted her skirt high enough to show freshly scraped up knees.

"What happened to your legs?"

Mal looked down at herself. "Oh, I've been biking a lot more. Training for a century ride. I lost my concentration and fell the other day." She pulled up her sleeve and showed far worse scrapes on her arms, one of them starting to fill with yellow pus. "It's not as bad as it looks. I forgot about it."

Laurie's gut cramped hard, nausea warring with concern. She brought out antiseptic ointment and sterilized a pair of tweezers.

"Sit."

"You're cute when you're bossy." Mal sat down on the couch with her wine.

Laurie dragged up a chair and turned on a lamp to see more clearly. In the yellow light, Mal's long curls reminded her of a lion's mane.

"Hold still," she said, reaching with the tweezers to pick out pieces of asphalt.

"You don't have to do this, you know," Mal said. "I've fallen plenty. Eventually the asphalt falls out."

"But if you take care of this properly, it won't scar."

Mal gave her a strange look.

"What?"

"Why do you care so much?"

Laurie didn't answer, afraid Mal would discover something she wasn't ready to admit, even to herself. She turned away to throw the debris into the trash. That night, she couldn't sleep, and by morning, she had a headache but woke up at the creaking of the hardwood floors.

She left the room to see Mal in bike gear.

"What's wrong?" she asked, sensing Mal's frustration.

"Period. It's not a problem on short rides, but a pad will shred to tatters on a longer ride, not to mention there's nothing in bike shorts to stick a pad to."

"Why not just use a tampon?"

For a long time Mal said nothing. Then she muttered, "I don't know how to insert a tampon."

Laurie blinked, uncertain how to process this information. Instinct warned her not to laugh. She went into the bathroom and showed Mal one of her own. Stripped it of its packaging and explained. "Once this part goes in, you just push—" She demonstrated how the cotton came loose from plastic. "Not rocket science, but it does feel like a miniature missile launch."

Mal's nose twitched. "What if—?"

Laurie waited.

"What if it goes in too deep and doesn't come out? Or if the thread snaps when I pull?"

She'd never known Mal to be unsure. Then she remembered how she'd had to learn this in the bathroom of a state park, with her mother explaining toxic shock while she stared at the dirty floor marked with wet, gray-brown footprints. How Mom had said, "I don't care how expensive they are. This isn't where you get cheap."

Laurie hadn't understood why she was telling her that until the house in Lansing, when Mom refused to replace a fifty-cent dish sponge for six months.

"There's nowhere for it to go," she reassured Mal. "I'll wait while you practice."

Mal went into the bathroom, and soon Laurie heard cursing.

"I broke it," Mal said.

"Open the door. How did you break a tampon?"

When the door opened Laurie caught sight of the plastic snapped in half and wrapped up in tissue. Her fingers rose to her lips. "Oh, *honey*. Be gentle." She gave Mal another tampon and showed her again.

"I hate these things," Mal said. Then she looked up. "Why do you look so pale?"

"Period," Laurie said, echoing her.

Mal grinned. "I guess we're in sync again."

Once she was gone, Laurie went into her room and leaned against the door, sliding down to the ground as she remembered how long it had been since Mal had asked her if they were out of sync. Her arms and legs trembled. Apparently she'd been bleeding, off and on, for the last twenty-five days.

She went to the doctor alone, glad she'd spent fifteen hours comparing Aetna, Cigna and Blue Shield against fifteen other insurance providers when the Unicorn first laid her off. Still, the only thing she could think about as she gave her insurance information was, *If it's cancer, I'll be broke.*

The gynecologist was supremely unhelpful, telling her fibroids were common in women her age, especially if they hadn't had children, before setting her back several hundred dollars for a biopsy and an ultrasound.

Great. Her parts were throwing a tantrum because she wasn't using them for their accepted purpose. And since a hysterectomy wasn't considered medically necessary, her choices were to wait it out or go for something called a UFE, which meant unidentified plastic sand flying around in her uterus.

She spent the rest of the day in bed, staring at the ceiling.

Mal came in to check on her. "Are you coming down with something?"

She shrugged.

"Well, I got you some sushi. Want to watch TV?"

Laurie did, but couldn't bring herself to get up. When she groaned, Mal came over to her bedside. Before she realized what Mal was doing, she'd reached one arm around Laurie's shoulders and another under her blanketed knees.

"You can't—I'm too heavy."

"You're the same size as my niece and nowhere near as wriggly."

Laurie stared in disbelief at the slowly approaching door, even as her arms locked behind Mal's neck. All she'd wished for was a hug. Now she was being princess-carried, blanket and all. The door was already open, but Mal toed it wide to let them through. Laurie held her breath until Mal deposited her on the couch. She was shocked by the unexpected gentleness from those strong arms. She couldn't pay attention to the TV after that, not when her skin burned from the remembered touch.

Some historical fantasy full of soft colors and French castles made her forget, for a while, the world of fibroids and health insurance claims and words like *myomectomy* and *embolization*. She fell asleep on the couch but woke up in her bed. She allowed herself two hot tears for not being awake to remember being carried back there.

A week later, the biopsy ruled out cancer, and Laurie cried until her lips bled from dehydration.

"You're definitely coming down with something," Mal said.

"Fibroids," she admitted, the relief over it *not* being cancer overwhelming any lingering shame.

"Oh, yeah I had one of those last year," Mal said. "It was hell on the way out."

She hadn't known.

"It was on a business trip to New York. I just pretended I was hungover."

"You kept working?"

Mal scoffed. "Can you imagine telling a room of guys who already ask if you're on the rag when you express the slightest emotion that you can't work on a critical deadline because of cramps?"

In that moment, two things became clear. First, Mal wasn't *incapable* of emotion. She'd just made a habit of hiding her feelings to survive her ridiculous world. Second, Laurie would get through this; she wasn't the first woman in the history of the world to deal with an overambitious blood clot.

• • •

She got a new job—well, the same admin job she'd had before—this time at the Darling. They were expanding, hiring so fast that people worked in the hallways, hunched cross-legged over laptops on the floors because there weren't enough desks. In the bathrooms were recruiting posters. *Know someone who'd be great for the team? We need fresh blood!*

Did they know how strange it was to be asking for fresh blood in the ladies' toilets? Probably not. It would be a few years before they'd notice such things. In 2010, women were called guys and didn't think anything of it, and the boys wore glitter and called each other girls, and seemed to like it.

Sophia had left the Darling, but Nick was back (idealism with the Obama campaign had not lasted against the frustration of government bureaucracy), and one day he asked Laurie, "I'm looking to date someone but only on weekends. Is that all right with you?"

At first she thought he was asking her general opinion on the subject, then realized he was actually asking her out, except in his head he'd already asked, and she'd already accepted. Something about that was both endearing and annoying, so she said yes before she remembered he'd dated Sophia and didn't know she had too. It rankled like an inherited debt—had Sophia ever truly acknowledged her, she wouldn't now feel she had to couple her own coming out with revealing what Sophia must have intended to keep secret.

She told Ariel about it, during one of their weekend burrito outings. Although she wasn't waitressing with her at Caliente anymore, she needed *normal* friends who weren't always going off to Burning Man or Maker Faire or Edwardian balls or blowing their thousand-dollar cash bonuses on truffle-and-champagne pasta and Paso Robles. Part of belonging was finding those you trusted to judge you when you deserved it.

"You don't think it's weird I dated his ex?"

"Of course it's weird," Ariel said. "But it's nowhere near the weirdest thing I've heard or even done."

That... didn't actually help her calibrate. Ariel might be her normal friend, but she had border-brown skin and waist-length hair the color of strawberries, and a tongue sharper than the Japanese knives she collected. And when she wasn't waitressing, she taught classes in BDSM at the Armory; Laurie had met her once coming off a night shift, and she sat in the coffee shop with her whip and paddle, serene to the point of disdain, a Venus in a leather corset and feather boa.

She'd had the same reaction then that she'd once had to Sophia—here was a woman who existed all the way, unapologetic and unashamed and colorful as the flowers and sunsets Laurie loved to paint. Shame always came first, but Ariel broke past it with a simple request—"Can you teach me how to invoice clients?"

Helping others, Laurie could do. Now they were friends.

"I don't know how others do it," Laurie said. "Pretend the past is another life, like it didn't even happen."

Ariel raised an eyebrow. Oh. That would've sounded pretty silly to someone who had just buried her past flyover-state self along with her deadname.

Laurie changed tack. "I've told you about Mal, right? That she hasn't so much as mentioned her ex Kas in months?"

"See, now that's weirder," Ariel said, poking a finger in her face. "The way you keep turning the subject to Mal."

Ariel was right. There were insurance claims to file, and a decision to be made about the increasingly unbearable pain from the fibroid that seemed to still be growing to the size of a grapefruit rather than shrinking away.

So yes, it was weird that the thing that bothered her the most was the strange way Mal was acting. Laurie was waiting for the other shoe to drop, and in the meantime, they had strained conversations about all the wrong things.

"Have you spoken to HR yet?" Mal asked her.

"Pain isn't a disability," she said. "And fibroids are an acute, not a chronic condition."

"Was that HR's assessment or yours?"

"I don't need medical leave."

"No, you need a long-term accommodation. Reduced working hours."

Laurie flinched. "It doesn't feel fair to make the same salary for less work."

"That's bullshit. It's the law."

One Tuesday night, Mal came home late, face flushed with happiness and inebriation.

"Laurie, you'll never guess," she called out from the bottom of the stairs.

"What?"

"I quit," Mal said, giggling. "The IPO, the waiting, it's all over."

For a moment, Laurie was certain she'd fallen down the stairs, the shock was so physical. Then, before she could react, Mal bounded upstairs, her long curly hair bouncing as if suddenly weightless.

"*Laurieeeee*." Mal picked her up and swung her around the living room in a circle. "I'm *freeeeee*."

Laurie laughed, unable to keep Mal's joy from affecting her, even while she reeled, *What will you do now? Where will you go?*

Mal was pacing, but it was a hyper, excited, skipping step with which she floated around the house, finding a champagne flute and filling it. She lost the filled glass on the way to the bathroom—"I left work early and had a round of drinks already to say goodbye, but I need to pee so badly"—filled a new glass before remembering, handed it to Laurie and then took it away, grabbed Laurie by the waist and pulled her close. "Oh, Laurie. We can do anything. We could go to the symphony every fucking day. Do you want a piano? I'll buy you a piano."

"Mal!" But her misgivings fell away under such wild, relentless joy.

Yes, her body sang. *Yes to anything, a thousand times.*

"I'm s-serious," Mal slurred, capering madly across the hardwood floor to find the errant champagne glass. "What would you like? Ask me anything."

Laurie brushed away a stray lock of curly hair from Mal's face. "I'm turning thirty this year," she said. "I don't want to spend it alone."

"Sure," Mal said. "Do you need me to disappear so you and... Nick, isn't it? You can have the place to yourselves."

"No, no boys. I want to go away with you. We could go to some fancy hotel? One with a pool. Maybe Tahoe? LA?"

"Hawaii? Fiji?"

"Hawaii," Laurie agreed, thinking they'd spend the summer planning so they could go around November.

They had tickets in an hour. They'd leave in five weeks. When Mal set her mind to something, no force on this earth could stop her.

. . .

Until then, Laurie filed insurance claims.

"Fibroid still bothering you?" Mal asked.

"Have you never filed insurance claims?" she snapped out. Her back hurt.

"No," Mal said. "My job took care of that. Huh. I guess I need to apply for health insurance now."

Of *course* Mal had never filed health insurance claims. *Her* body spat out fibroids like they were chewed up tobacco. The woman was training for a century ride, and carried the whole damn bike on her shoulder up and down the stairs and through the BART station gate.

Getting out of bed was getting harder. Laurie fought a war of attrition with her fibroid, trying to choose between getting the UFE and waiting for the coarse plastic sand to shrivel the damn things, or spending several thousand dollars on a hysterectomy. In her delirious state she had conversations with Ariel in her head. Offered up her uterus at a discount, except Ariel had already bought one from Best Buy for less.

The more Laurie withdrew from social life, the more obsessed Nick became. She made delicate excuses not to see him, but he dragged her to fancy restaurants and plied her with Swarovski. One Saturday morning, he called to ask if she wanted to drive to Napa. Too exhausted to care how it came across, she said simply, "Can't. Cramps."

She dragged herself to the bathroom, leaning against the wall when her vision blurred. The tile was so cool and inviting. She curled up on the floor, back to the wall, head near the toilet bowl. She was sweating from the pain, body shaking with it, and she could *feel* the clot worming its way through the tiny tunnel. Her body was gnawing at it, forcing it out, each contraction forcing her to clutch the bathmat in agony while sparks flew behind her eyelids.

"Laurie?" Mal's voice was tremulous. So frightened and far away.

A warm, wet towel made its way to Laurie's lower back, shifting her pelvis into a more comfortable position. An icepack landed on her forehead. She clutched the bathmat feverishly and waited.

"Drink this," Mal said, lifting her neck so a little bit of orange-flavored water could make its way down her throat. "Electrolytes."

The thing inside Laurie moved. One day, she was going to name this fucker.

"I'm all right now." She ushered Mal out of the bathroom, pulled down her underwear and sat on the toilet. There was a give, and then a slow, slick and satisfying slide. Something landed with a splash.

Laurie exhaled in relief. Then another cramp followed, sharper and more intense than any so far. It was crippling, and she wasn't braced for it. She screamed in agony and passed out.

• • •

She woke up in the hospital. Mal yanked the curtain aside, looking murderous.

"They won't tell me anything," she said. "I'm not family."

It turned out there was more than one cyst—of course, with Laurie's luck, there would be—and while one had shrunk the other had grown, and would she consider—

"Yes," she said immediately. "Hysterectomy. Take it all out."

Mal whirled around, stunned.

"The other option," the doctor said delicately, "is less permanent."

"You'll never have children," Mal said.

God, she loved how direct Mal was. It was such a comfort, when everything else seemed uncertain and complicated.

"And I'll never have another period either."

Once the doctor was gone, she pinched Mal's skirt to get her to come closer.

"How did I get here?"

"Ambulance."

"How much did it cost?"

"Jesus, shut up. I should've seen it. I'm so, so sorry."

"You're here now. Can you find my phone and text Nick?"

"I already did," Mal said. "He's sent flowers."

But he hadn't come. It was a weekday. Laurie was more surprised by her lack of disappointment.

Mal sat down heavily in an uncomfortable-looking plastic chair by the side of her bed. For a single, strange moment, Laurie was reminded of her brother Jack, who really only wanted the kind of problem he could hit with a shovel. Mal wasn't much different, although her choice of shovel was usually a credit card.

"Hey Mal?"

She snapped to guilty attention.

"Can I have some ice-cream?"

Laurie had the feeling Mal needed work to stay sane, and that she'd rather take care of someone than face whatever demons she'd been running from when she quit her job. The quantity of salted caramel ice-cream she brought over from Bi-Rite told Laurie she was right.

Suddenly her heart started pounding.

"What is it?" Mal asked.

"Hawaii," she said. "We were supposed to go next weekend, but now I'll be in surgery, and it'll probably be a month before I can get on a plane." A lump formed in her throat, as the Tahoe trip with Adam loomed in her memory.

"Oh," Mal said, relaxing into her chair. "Is that all? I'll move the bookings, or cancel them if you prefer."

I love you, Laurie thought, and then panicked so hard she had a coughing fit.

Fuck. I'm in love with you.

• • •

In Hilo, a cruise-ship deposited its load in front of them; two dozen retirees stormed the tiny restaurant where they sat. The men wore Polynesian shirts and dresses, and the women wore complimentary orchids pinned on their extra-large t-shirts. Laurie glanced self-consciously at her own arms and shoulders. They'd probably never turn into leathery, lobster-colored saddlebags, but artificial knees might be just ten years away.

"You're quiet," Mal said.

Laurie shrugged. She wasn't the one keeping secrets. There was something Mal wasn't telling her, something more to the sudden financial windfall that had allowed her to quit the Unicorn without having another job lined up.

Or maybe she was trying to pick a fight to diffuse the sudden and inconvenient feelings she'd just discovered. Living the romcom life, tropes and all.

"I hate cruise ships," Mal said. "If you're done eating, let's get out of here."

"There's a black sand beach, about twenty miles down."

Mal pulled over behind a long line of cars, grabbed her sunscreen and camera and headed out, and Laurie followed. Mal was solicitous as they headed down the rocky passageway to the hidden black-sand enclave. It had been two months since the surgery but Mal still treated her as if she were made of glass. Not that she was going to complain.

The beach was nestled in the elbow of a cliff, and the smell of marijuana and incense overpowered the ocean spray. Two men were beatboxing, and around them a cabal of women danced naked. Other naked men and women sprinted into the waves and fell back laughing into each other's arms. Laurie paused. The surgical scar was well-hidden by her bikini, but these people's nudity called up her body's recent failings.

"You going to swim?" Mal asked.

"It's cold."

A young nude woman with small, upturned breasts walked out of the sea with flecks of black sand between her legs. She lay down on her back, one knee raised, drawing her fingers elaborately through the sand near her thighs, and then lazily flicked off the sand, one particle at a time. Laurie couldn't take her eyes off her long, perfect legs, the tanned glow of her skin, the inviting dark sand between her legs.

It had been nearly two years since she'd felt the lick of arousal, so she almost didn't recognize it underneath her envy. She stared at her own thighs, on which cellulite formed a gentle honeycomb. Thirty was when you knew your skin was never really going to clear up, when you discovered there was such a thing as back fat.

The naked woman on the beach turned onto her stomach, legs parted to allow the sea foam to tease her. Flecks of dark sand slid off her with each wave's caress. With difficulty, Laurie tore her eyes away and looked for Mal, who was climbing the rocks of the far cliff, trying to reach an impossible vantage point. Naturally.

Mal reached the crag and waved, and Laurie waved back. On the way down she was caught off guard by a wave and fell about ten feet into the sand. It must have hurt, but she simply got up and walked back.

"Are you hurt?'

"Just a scrape. It was so much fun though, you should've come."

Mal always said these things thoughtlessly. *You should've come*, as if there was no place she could go that Laurie couldn't follow. As if the only thing holding her back was a lack of interest.

"Those women were beautiful," she said in the car as they drove away. "Especially the brunette with the tattoos on her ankles."

"Curly hair, lying on the sand next to your rock?"

"She was like a pixie."

"You're cuter," Mal said.

"My breasts don't stand up."

"They're bigger."

"Okay," she said, to end the conversation. In the rearview mirror, her ears were lava-red.

At Hawaii Paradise Park, where they'd be staying, the night was so loud that the sound of the car locking was drowned out by the trilling of coqui frogs.

The next day was foggy. Rain peppered the windshield. Mal turned off the radio with an annoyed click when five stations in a row played pop music or Christian rock. The car hissed solitarily along the wet, sinuous road. The leaves of the palms and sedge were large with yellow blades for tips, at once suggestive and predatory. The climbing fern were green with copper blades, the fiddleheads larger than a fist.

"I believe the fiddleheads are called *uluhe*," Mal said. "The shorter fern is the *ama'u*. It's unique to Hawaii. The red fronds are used as dye."

Laurie smiled to herself. She'd just expressed a wish yesterday to know their names. Of course Mal had taken on a research project.

It was too wet for hikers, so they were the only ones on the *Halema'uma'u* trail. The tropical rain-forest yielded abruptly to a desolate, lunar landscape of jagged lava rock. Less than a mile away, the active crater sent up an enormous plume. Thin, yellowish-white trails of sulfur led to deep fissures from which hot steam rose. The birds of the forest could no longer be heard.

She'd chosen Hawaii imagining beaches and pineapples, and now they were walking on a crater, a bare mile from a thrashing lava pit. Did anything define America so much as false advertising? How many people came to Northern California lured by its many false promises—warm weather, sandy beaches, flexible working hours? Maybe they were all hustlers, and the only way to fall in love with America was to exploit it.

"Cold?"

"I'm fine," she lied, savagely glad Mal had noticed her involuntary shivering.

"I'm starving. Let's head back."

After lunch they headed to Ka Lae, the southernmost point of the United States. Several bouncy miles down a barely-paved road they found the dregs of industrialization, some broken and rusted pipes, balls of barbed wire, and cliffs formed by benches of lava crashing into the ocean.

"This is it?" Mal asked. "I'd expected a National Park, a beach, something. Instead we have some detritus, Port-a-potties, and a dude selling junk out of his SUV."

"This is America, baby," Laurie said. "There's always someone trying to make a buck."

Mal threw her head back and laughed, that deep, rumbling sound Laurie had only heard once in the mountains of Tahoe.

Her belly warmed to hear it. *I did that.*

Then, as Mal walked toward the edge of the cliff, she hung back, the warning stuck in her throat. She saw the wooden plank that jutted out over the cliff at the same time Mal did.

"Mal, no," she called out preemptively.

She turned around, the grin reaching her ears. "Mal, *yes*."

"You aren't seriously going to jump off a cliff of lava into the Pacific ocean."

"Hold the camera. You'd better take pictures."

Within seconds, she'd taken a gleeful and glorious leap, landing with a loud splash into the deep blue below. Laurie lay down on the ground and looked over the edge with held breath to seek her out when she surfaced, heart pounding against the rock beneath her chest.

Mal surfaced, waved and climbed up the ladder, but it wasn't until they were back on asphalt that Laurie could breathe. They got in the car and headed up north again, to spend the night in a resort cottage by the beach.

"I got you something," Laurie confessed, once they were settled into the cottage and unpacked.

"Why am I getting the gifts? Also, I didn't get you anything."

"You got me this whole trip. " Laurie brought out the bike shorts she'd bought.

"Thank you."

"Look inside."

Inside the shorts, she'd sewn a lining using the material from sanitary pads.

"It's not reusable, but probably good for a century ride."

Mal didn't say anything. It made her nervous.

"You get it? You took care of my lady parts, I'm trying to take care of yours?" Still no answer. "Mal, what is it?"

"I remember the day I told you about this. You weren't well. Even back then, and I didn't notice."

"I wasn't ready for you to."

A beat. Finally Mal said, with what could almost pass for nervousness, "I got you something too. But before I give it to you, there's a secret. Something I haven't told anyone."

Laurie's stomach sank with dread.

"No, don't worry, it's nothing like that. It's just a bit embarrassing. You remember how you said my writing career was stuck because all people really wanted to read about was hot people being stupid?"

"That was a joke."

"You weren't wrong." Mal inhaled deeply. "I've been writing romance. Under a pen-name. I self-published on a whim, and… well, it turns out there are a *lot* of people who want to read the stuff. Who knew they'd pay for it? It's not much, but… your advice more than paid for this vacation."

If *Not much* could pay for flights and a luxury resort, Laurie wondered what Mal's idea of *expensive* was. So far she hadn't discovered it.

She asked if she could read it and Mal said no without hesitating.

"It's crap. But I did want to share something else I wrote." Mal handed her a notebook, one she'd seen her carry on all their road trips along the coast to jot down ideas and journal her thoughts. "I've copied out the notes if I decide to do something about them, but I wanted you to have the original."

Mal kept her face turned away from her as she readied for bed, as if worried about what Laurie might think. As if there was a single thought in her mind beyond, *You're trusting me with your drafts.*

She read the entire notebook that very night, then returned to one particular passage:

I want to live my life in baroque—moving, always moving, driving miles in an almost ravenous conquest of expanse, discovering indescribable ecstasies that exhaust every sense and thought. Such perfect moments are accompanied by a shattering so complete I'm left only with a burning, consuming faith in my capacity for happiness. Can't chug along, complacent and numb, chasing after sunk costs and shadows, not when L won't let me lie.

She mouthed the last sentence silently, her fingers clutching the sheets.

The next day, they rolled down to breakfast at a table overlooking the ocean. Mal ordered champagne and coffee without even thinking about it, as if there was no question this was how one ought to live out any day, not just birthdays.

"Are you working on anything new?" Laurie asked.

"I've got two ideas, not sure which one I like more. The first is about two guys who are roommates in college, who end up getting drunk and kissing in Mexico on Spring Break. Everything gets super awkward until they get their act together in time for a climax of cathartic sex."

Mal had clearly meant to make her laugh, but Laurie winced, recognizing the inspiration immediately.

Her face fell. "You don't like it."

"I'm still mad at myself for never seeing it. Cam and Will."

Laurie went to get a second round of food from the buffet before the breakfast closed. She wondered if her foolishness might now be laid bare to the world through Mal's words. It was why she'd never painted anyone but Sophia. Landscapes were easier—loving them said nothing about her.

She came back with a Belgian waffle with ice-cream and asked, "What's the other idea?"

"It's based on my sister before she got married. I guess you don't know how we grew up. My dad liked us to be independent, free thinkers. But it meant that when we went back to India for the summers, we didn't fit in *at all*."

Mal had never talked about her father before.

"Everything was a debate at the dinner table. We couldn't just like *The Lion King*. We had to provide commentary on the portrayal of unsustainable consumption in Scar's destruction of the Pridelands. One summer, my sister met someone." Mal's eyes drifted to the ocean. "I was very young, and I didn't understand what I saw. I never knew his name. To me, he was only the Coconut Man, who came to cut the branches sometimes. Just one of the many servants and cooks and chauffeurs. Until Aditi made him visible."

Her world was so strange to Laurie, and yet she couldn't help but understand. She was no main character, but she knew all too well what it meant to be plucked out of obscurity by one. Made visible.

"Anyway," Mal continued, "after I saw them together, after I *understood*, he was unforgettable. Beautiful. A panther with a machete over whom my sister exerted complete command with only a look or a word."

"Your sister doesn't seem like the type," Laurie said carefully.

"She was different then. We all were, before…" She took a long sip of her champagne, and Laurie understood. *Before our father died.* "She was kind of an activist. She'd been reading a lot of Arundhati Roy, and she wanted to shatter caste and gender taboos. I think the guy scratched her twin itches for adolescent rebellion and Maoist revolution."

"So you'd write about your sister and this guy?"

"What does it say that when I imagine her happy, she'd be divorced from her current husband or having a torrid affair with the Coconut Man while her kids are off at Kumon?"

"Probably that you're still angry about how they treated you when you were living with them."

"I forgot you knew about that." She looked out at the ocean. "Let's go surf."

Laurie didn't want to surf, as she was still shaky after her surgery, but she convinced Mal to go ahead. She was driven to draw, especially when Mal walked out of the waves looking like Pele, the volcanic goddess herself, shining and dark-eyed, as if she could contain all of the earth's fury. Her hair had grown long with unemployment, and it hung wet and curly on her shoulders, with tiny drops of water trembling from the tips before slipping down to disappear between her breasts.

Laurie passed her a bottle of water when she came ashore. Mal shook her head, but she held her arm out insistently until Mal drank.

"So bossy." Mal's lips twitched with amusement.

"You know it," Laurie said, and held out the sunscreen next. Mal groaned, but took it.

"If you can see, there's UV," she said sweetly. When she'd first met Mal, the woman had been operating under the illusion that her darker skin required no care.

"You made me look strong," Mal said upon seeing the sketch she'd made of her. "Like an Amazon warrior."

"You do know that's how you look, right?"

"I know. My mom always said I had the shoulders of a man."

Laurie was the one without a uterus and *Mal* was the one who felt unfeminine.

"Well, mothers do that—pass on their fear and pain as our inheritance."

"That's... wise."

"I'd love to be more spontaneous," Laurie said. "But I also can't silence her voice in my head telling me to pick a Roth IRA over romance."

"Laurie," Mal said incredulously, "you're the most spontaneous, *present* person I know. You see everything, every ugly painting in hotels and hallways, every flicker of emotion on anyone's face. Everyone else is a stale, artificial neon light vying for scraps of attention, but you're a fire that could consume them if they dared to look away."

Her mouth opened and closed. She wanted to laugh it off, but then there was *L won't let me lie*. Maybe Mal wouldn't let her laugh this off either.

She needed Mal to look away, to do *something*, because her palms burned and her face was on fire and she was going to cry.

"You're like an affogato," Mal said. "Vanilla at first glance, but bitter, strong and dark coffee deep down."

Laurie fell off the ledge laughing. It was only hours later, after they'd played in the waves and lounged by the pool, when they stumbled home giggling after far too many piña coladas, that she realized she was supposed to have been on a call with Nick, but had forgotten about him entirely.

Guilt trickled down her spine like ice-water at his *Worried about you, hope everything's okay! Happy birthday! Love you!*

Her fingers stilled on the phone keyboard.

"Hey, Mal?"

"Yeah?" came a voice from the bathroom.

"How do you know when love is real?"

Mal was silent for a long time. She emerged, brushing tangles out of her hair. "I don't know," she said softly. "I don't know that I've ever felt it. Sometimes I *want* to believe it's real, but that's not good enough. I want to be *forced* to believe. To feel so much that there's no room for doubt."

Baroque, she'd written.

Laurie thought of Sophia, dreaming of dragging her Manolo Blahniks through the mud. Of Ian, who had come to San Francisco with nothing but the clothes on his back, just for the *possibility* of finding the love that dared not speak its name in right-wing America. Of Kerouac and Cassady, who loved each other so much they set fire to an entire generation.

"You want rapture," she said, "experience that can withstand the onslaught of language."

"Yes," Mal said, eyes wide with wonder. "I don't want to *choose* to stay. I want it to be unthinkable to leave."

Their eyes met. And held. Laurie swallowed.

And looked away.

Sorry, lost track of the timezone difference. Love you too, she typed to Nick.

Nearly five times she tried to add an exclamation point, and failed.

chapter eight

by 2011, the Darling had grown so large that when Mal eventually started working there, it was in another building. Laurie never saw her. They went to work together on the BART, setting up a daily routine that involved picking up coffee and waffles at the Bluebottle in the Ferry Building by the Embarcadero. For twenty minutes each morning they watched the boats cross the bay, listened to seagulls wail, and talked about anything, everything.

"Nick wants me to pick the restaurant next time," Laurie said. "He thinks my notions of gender roles are archaic. Is it so wrong that given my job, I want a break from making decisions?"

Mal nodded contemplatively. "You can try telling him we've come full-circle, so now the man making all the moves is a rare and subversive kink. He's actually a true feminist, letting you let him dominate."

Laurie swatted at her, told her the name of the place she'd been considering, an Italian one up in North Beach, and asked her opinion.

"Last time I was there, I had the Zucchini fiori, but I went home with the waiter. Not as good as the zucchini."

"Nick isn't the most skilled in bed, but I'm sure he can outperform a vegetable."

Mal sighed. "We have high standards for soup, but not for sex."

Laurie didn't bother contradicting her. The issues with Nick weren't his fault. She hadn't been able to climax since her surgery. Hadn't even touched herself between her legs except when she needed to treat a yeast infection. She understood why so many women didn't want their husbands in the room during childbirth; it was hard to hold onto desire in the face of biological reality.

They separated to enter their office buildings. Laurie served as admin to a new Director bent on restructuring his team and cultivating the next generation of leaders. He was completely unaware that his team spent their nights on absinthe and karaoke, that they didn't have the money for rent so they lived in cars or in RVs parked outside Daly City, or that they had no idea what he was talking about but just parroted the words he said—*push the envelope, shift the paradigm, pave the cow path*—whichever would let them believe themselves safe from the next round of layoffs.

The pundits gave their generation a name—*millennials*—and wrote articles about how they'd survived the Great Recession, but those writers never quite understood what it meant to not feel even the *pain* of a lost future. Even sadness seemed out of reach when pensions were a notion as quaint as chamberpots, when 401Ks were worthless, when all they had left was the gig economy, dystopian novels and Twitter, snatches of life that never built up to anything. They'd refused it all, nostalgia and anxiety, history and hope, in favor of an effervescent, breathless present.

Nick asked Laurie to move in with him. "It just doesn't make sense to pay two rents in this market."

This was what she'd always wanted, wasn't it? A practical proposal. Except it wasn't a proposal.

"I guess I always figured I'd be engaged first," she said.

"Marriage doesn't make sense if we're not going to have kids, does it?"

She stared at him. Their various possible futures suddenly started playing out in her head. They moved in together, lived happily for five years, and then he left her for a woman with a uterus when he decided he really did want kids. They moved in together, got in each other's way, and tired of it within the year. At no point did she consider the possibility that they might live together into old age. Hope like that was impractical at best, foolish at worst.

"California divorce laws aren't fair," Nick said. "All marital assets are divided fifty-fifty, regardless of who paid what share. That makes sense if there are kids involved, but otherwise..."

Otherwise it meant that he, as the higher earner, would relinquish half his assets—cash savings, stocks in the Darling, a house they might buy—to her.

A stone lodged in her stomach. *This* was what it meant to be a millennial, to plan for the eventuality of the destruction of all her dreams. To believe they had to continually earn their place in each other's lives, like corporations beholden to a board of shareholders.

"But if we move in together and it doesn't work out," she began, slowly, "my apartment's rent-controlled. Once I move out, my landlord will raise the rent, because it's my name on the lease."

He nodded, taking no offense. If she moved in with him and

it didn't work out, she'd be homeless.

"Well, I suppose there's no harm in carrying on as we have been," he said. "I'm happy, if you are."

. . .

"He's a shifty little grifter," Ariel said when Laurie met up with her. They were in a converted yoga studio in the mission where hipsters with hair all colors of the rainbow met to discuss the ills of capitalism and the necessity of a labor movement. "Men like him honestly believe that women who stay at home to take care of kids are freeloaders."

Laurie shifted on her feet. At work, her manager had told her she was clearly in line for a promotion, especially since she wouldn't be disappearing at a critical time on maternity leave.

"I'm all about equal pay for equal work," he'd said, "but you can't have your cake and eat it too."

For a moment, she'd actually believed him. Then Ariel tore into her for days, and demanded she join her underground labor collective.

So during the week Laurie spent her days helping introverted engineers discover their leadership skills by attempting to herd sheep—actual sheep! that she rented for their workshop!—and her nights listening to the building fury of the disenfranchised proletariat.

On the weekends, she hung out with Nick, learned to watch his favorite shows—Battlestar Galactica, Firefly, Stargate Atlantis—and tried not to wonder if he'd know how to navigate the health insurance market if she got sick, or if he could only access real life emotions when they were filtered through the lens of space opera.

Still, she *should* have been happy. She had a stable job, a loyal boyfriend, and more than one thousand dollars in the bank.

Just no orgasm.

And California was a cure for all ills, a cult sampler, a veritable buffet of leadership skills and bedroom techniques.

"You win or lose in your mind before you even enter the field," said the leadership coach her Director had brought in this month to tease out entrepreneurship from a gaggle of gun-shy geeks, just as, "Arousal is about mental focus, not physical skill," said the pleasure coach at the seminar on Relationship Anti-patterns.

So it was her mind that was the problem, and mindfulness was the answer. Stanford had used MRIs to image the brains of Tibetan monks; now tech companies wanted to leverage artificial intelligence to build emotional intelligence. Fifty years after Ken Kesey attempted to take everyone *further* by expanding people's consciousness with LSD, leadership coaches and orgasmic meditation coaches and therapists attempted to do the same—this time with CBT or CBD.

Nick was surprisingly enthusiastic when she brought it up. Maybe a pleasure coach carried less baggage than the idea of couples therapy, or it spoke to his scientific curiosity and need to decode the female orgasm. Laurie offered to pay for it; all he had to do was show up.

The pleasure coach sat cross-legged by a nest of pillows and blankets, and asked her to undress from the waist down, as if she were setting up for a pelvic exam. Laurie followed the instructions and butterflied her legs, shivering at the cool air against her exposed skin. Nick sat to her right with a dollop of gel on his poised forefinger, an attentive student in the art of female pleasure.

For fifteen minutes—they had a timer, and an app—they had only to focus on one thing. Her.

Laurie's mind raced. She wanted to laugh. She and Nick had left work early today to come here. She really was using her flextime on this, when Ariel was scrounging for her bottom surgery, when the homeless encampments near their office had started to add urine to the smell of sewage.

No, she had to focus, get her money's worth. No need to drown in that peculiar guilt that haunted those of them who had survived the recession. They'd been forced to pick between happiness and survival; the only revenge was living well.

Her eyes fell on Nick. They'd been dating nearly two years, but somehow in that moment, in that aggressively pink light meant to stimulate the reluctant feminine, he seemed a complete stranger.

Panicked, she tried reminding herself of how well he knew her, how he'd always picked the right jewelry and restaurants, how he remembered her birthday and the names of her siblings, how neatly their routines had dovetailed, how they'd never had a single fight.

"Her heart rate's increasing," said the coach approvingly. "Did you notice? That's a good signal to continue what you're doing."

Right, because his finger was... oh god. The intense pin-prick burn grew unbearable, her toes curled, her muscles clenched—

"She's close. Learn to recognize the signs. Stay the course."

—but there was no release. Instead, she started convulsing against the pillows, her upper body thrashing in distress. Too much! She pushed Nick's hand away, moaned in pain.

"All right. Take a break. She's overstimulated."

"That's good, isn't it?" Nick asked, his body turned toward

the coach.

"It's… progress. Laurie, you say this has been going on for two years?"

"Since her surgery," Nick said confidently, although they hadn't even started sleeping together until after Hawaii.

Later, he put his arm around her and patted her shoulder. "It's not the end of the world. We made progress today. We'll keep trying."

He seemed glad of a problem to solve, as if she was a kitchen to be renovated. He packaged her into an Uber and sent her home.

There was a young girl sitting on her doorstep. As she got closer, the girl's head lifted. Laurie recognized the dark skin, high cheekbones and curly hair immediately.

"I'm Tara," said the girl, putting out her hand. "When does my aunt usually get home?"

"Laurie," she said.

The girl nodded impatiently. "Yeah, I know you from Facebook. Can you let me in? It's freezing out here."

Laurie opened the door, wondering where she'd come from and what she was doing here in San Francisco without a jacket.

"It was warm and sunny in the South Bay," Tara said. "I came here on the Caltrain, then took the BART from Millbrae."

"Yeah, microclimates. San Francisco's always cold. Does Mal know you're coming?"

"I texted her."

"Mal doesn't check her phone while she's at work, but she should be here soon." She looked Tara over uneasily. She was so tiny! "Do your parents know you're here?"

Tara scowled. "No. I'd hardly be running away if I told them where I was going, would I?"

Laurie hesitated, unsure what to do next. "Would you like to talk about it?"

"I'm saving it for the therapist."

What a punk!

"Well, do you want something to eat?"

"What do you have? I'm vegan."

Of course she was. Laurie brought out some hummus and crackers, and turned to get a plate, but when she turned back Tara had already started eating it out of the box.

"So, are you like her roommate, or—" Tara made air-quotes— "her *roommate*?"

"I have a boyfriend."

Tara shrugged. "Auntie Mal's loaded, and she hates people, so why would she live with you instead of getting her own place?"

Laurie's mouth opened and closed. She wanted to say, *She's probably saving up*, except that didn't sound like Mal at all. The woman combined a lack of impulse control with a seemingly bottomless bank account, and there were three-hundred dollar shoes strewn all over the landing because the closets were too full.

"Well, Mal's straight," she said.

Tara snorted. "She's many things; straight isn't one of them."

"How would you know?" she said, unable to keep the ice out of her voice.

"When she was in college, she told my mom that she wasn't sure she wanted to get married because she was attracted to women."

"What did your mom say?"

"Something about how women's bodies are just more attractive, and nobody was *actually* attracted to men." Tara paused to wipe up the last of the hummus with her finger. "Mom lied, though. After the call ended, she called my grandma and had a total meltdown."

"And she—they talked about all this in front of you?"

Tara rolled her eyes. "They thought I wouldn't understand. But I was eight, not stupid."

A key turned in the lock downstairs. Laurie's heart started pounding. She wanted to run to her room to hide. How could Mal not have told her? (It didn't occur to her then that she'd never told Mal about Sophia, either).

Mal came upstairs and sighed theatrically upon seeing Tara, but the smile at the edge of her lips gave her away. "I guess I should be glad you came north to me instead of trying to go south to Mexico."

"I only had twenty bucks. Mom won't let me have a bank account."

Mal turned to Laurie. "Thanks for keeping her company."

She told Mal it was no trouble and took her words as dismissal because she needed to escape. She went into her room and shut the door, threw herself onto the bed.

What a day! The earlier convulsions from the pleasure coaching session were nothing to the way her heart was palpitating now.

How dare that little brat make her feel the prick of hope?

· · ·

"I've said I'm fine," Tara said into her phone, sounding more tired the next morning than she had last night.

Mal put her fingers over her lips. It was Saturday, and they moved silently in their usual weekend routines. A sizzle from the stove said Mal was making breakfast, so Laurie started to set the dining table.

"Mom... *Mom*, if you aren't going to listen, I'm going to hang up."

Mal motioned to her, and the two women went into Laurie's room. "I'm thinking of taking her for a drive today. Clear her head a bit, maybe get her to open up about what's actually going on. Can you come with?"

"I'm not family."

"People open up around you."

Yes, but the qualities that made Laurie a receptacle for every awkward engineer's feelings weren't likely to work the same on a teenage Gen Z mutineer.

"I know it's asking a lot, and you usually spend weekends with Nick." Mal turned to go.

"Wait. We could make a weekend of it. Find a place to stay along the coast? Then if she wants to be alone with you, I could disappear."

Mal pulled her into a quick, hard hug, whispering *thank you*. She pulled out her phone and extended the Zipcar booking. "It'll be like old times. I've been going stir-crazy."

She needs me. We're just friends.

Laurie sent an apology to Nick and started packing an overnight bag. She couldn't lie to herself anymore. Electricity ran through her fingers while she packed her pajamas. She couldn't stop grinning, like one of those people on the subway whose minds had been shot through with drugs.

Stir-crazy? Was that what she ought to call the arousal in her gut at the thought of a drive down the coast? She could already feel the sunshine on her arm, lodged on the open window.

She'd have to pull rank on Tara. No way the brat was taking shotgun.

They headed north, towards Mendocino, trying and failing

to be good role models for the kid in the back seat. It didn't help that Tara had no filter.

"How did you both lose your virginity?"

Mal started laughing.

"You can't just *ask* people that," Laurie said.

"Your generation is so squeamish."

"You hear that?" Mal drawled. "*This* is what comes of letting the Russians take LiveJournal. Now their generation thinks they invented sex, like we weren't fantasizing about vampires when they were conceived."

"Fine then." Laurie folded her arms. "In a car, under an overpass, near a soy farm."

"That's a terrible start to a story," Tara said. "You're supposed to focus on who it was with."

"I'm getting to that. We ancients are used to starting our stories with a description of the times and a paragraph of world-building context. Not everything fits in a tweet."

Tara huffed.

Laurie closed her eyes. She could still see signs along the thin highway for *George Bush 2000* interspersed with *NO FRACKING* and *FUCK MONSANTO*. There were farms of soy on the hills, small and squat creatures that had sucked the soil dry and now rested with their fat beans hanging in clumps like hard, green testicles.

"Soy is a ruthless survivor," Diana had said, holding her close. "Just like us. You can't help but admire it, even when you hate it."

"Us?" she asked.

Diana turned to her, her lovely face a study in anguish. "You know we can never do this again, right?"

"She was a musician," Laurie said, and Mal's head jerked

up. She returned to her usual steadiness so quickly Laurie wouldn't have noticed if she hadn't been looking for it. "We'd been playing together a while, so we were... attuned."

Diana was other things too. Married, with kids. And a Teacher's Assistant in the class she was auditing at Cornell, one who hid the fact that Laurie wasn't really a student. At the time she thought she did it out of love. Now, she wondered if Diana only hid her secrets because she hid hers, if it had all been transactional. "But our timing was never really as good in real life as it was in our music."

Tara paused for a moment, longer than usual, but went on so nonchalantly it felt as if maybe there hadn't been any silence, after all. "Auntie? What about you?"

"I was late to the party. I'd always lived at home, I didn't get out much in college, and then I came to live with you."

"And if Mom so much as sees fancy lingerie she thinks you're selling yourself on street corners," Tara said sulkily.

Laurie exchanged a glance with Mal, glad of the clue.

"I decided to be rid of it once and for all," Mal went on. "Too much hype about making your first time special, when all the data suggests you're not going to make your first relationship a success. I found a guy at work I thought was cute, one who was going to quit so I wouldn't have to work with him after. I kissed him and asked him to take me home, just for the night. He was a good teacher, and he made me breakfast burritos the next morning, so that was a bonus."

"*Will?* You gave your virginity to Will?" Then the full implications hit her. "That was the night we met."

Beyond that was an even wilder outrage. It wasn't fair that such an undeserving cad had managed to get not just Cam's virginity but Mal's too.

"I wanted to see what the fuss was about," Mal said.

"And did you?" She couldn't keep the bitterness out of her voice.

"Yes and no." Mal drummed her fingers on the steering wheel. "I'd heard so many horror stories, about how sex changes your body chemistry, how you can't help but feel an emotional attachment afterwards. He was a little worried about that too—that I'd turn clingy and want a relationship. But it wasn't like that. It felt good, but also…"

"Also?" Tara asked.

"It felt like a warm-up," Mal said. "I don't think sex is ever great the first time, so it felt like practice for when I meet someone who might want to get better at it with me over time."

Tara looked contemplative, and Laurie could guess at what might have happened to send the girl spinning. Mal wouldn't have revealed so much if she hadn't guessed first.

Sure enough, later that night, when they settled into adjoining rooms at a coastal inn, Mal came over after Tara was asleep to tell her, "Aditi found condom wrappers in the trash and freaked out."

"It's understandable. My mom had Micah when she was Tara's age. She never finished high school, and her parents disowned her."

"My grandparents never disowned my mother, but they never forgave her for my father either. It still eats at her."

Laurie waited for her to explain.

"He was a lot like you, actually." Mal laughed nervously. "Followed his heart. Graduated Harvard, chose to teach high-school kids because he felt he was making a difference. Everyone else thought he was a failure and told him so. When he died… well, wisdom doesn't pay the bills."

Their eyes caught again. Laurie couldn't forget what Tara had told her. *So, your niece says you might be into women. Any women in particular?*

No, why would Mal—who cowed rooms of men into submission with a look, and took home waiters and baristas with a word—be suddenly indirect and hesitant about this?

"I should go," Mal said, but didn't move.

Laurie's phone beeped. Both sets of eyes turned to the message from Nick, checking in dutifully on Tara's well-being.

Mal got up and left the room.

. . .

The next morning, the crisp ocean breeze left Laurie dizzy, too blazed by the shimmer of sapphire blue to think of anything else. They passed through the tiny one-street towns of Point Arena and Gualala, and marveled, hushed, at the dark rocks in Bodega Bay that seemed to be crumbled Oreos at the bottom of treacherous cliffs. As the sun started to set, Tara fell asleep, and Laurie fixed her eyes on Mal.

She'd never been more aroused than on that drive, with the hum of the car engine on an empty road in the rapacious darkness, and that reckless, ruinous smile Mal gave her sometimes, matched only by the sunset, and the open sea.

chapter nine

their acquired teenager slotted so tidily into their lives that when Mal said, "I think we ought to let your mom at least know where you are, don't you?" Laurie counted the days in her head and was surprised that they added up to more than two weeks.

"She knows I'm alive and safe," Tara said, scowling. "If she can't respect my boundaries, I won't live with her. I'm headed off to college in a month anyway. You of all people ought to understand."

Mal threw Laurie a hesitant look.

"Unless I'm in your way," Tara said, catching the glance.

"You're not an inconvenience," Laurie said firmly.

She really wasn't. Tara slept on an air-mattress in the living room, but unless Laurie woke up in the middle of the night to use the bathroom, she'd never know the girl was there. She cleared up after herself, even removing her toothbrush into Mal's room each morning and washing every dish immediately after she used it.

Laurie wanted to tell her about living with her mother and two brothers in the back of a car, during those uncomfortable years when they thought farts were the funniest thing ever and she was just getting her period. But she didn't. Maybe it was the easy way Tara called herself *possibly queer, definitely questioning*, using words Laurie had never had at that age, and now that they were available to her, felt by turns too unwieldy or volatile to use, at least in talking about herself. Or maybe it was the way Tara's mood could pendulum-swing in an instant between self-righteousness—*If you don't pay Dolores enough for benefits, you shouldn't keep a maid*—to self-recrimination—*You shouldn't listen to an entitled princess with a trust fund.*

That summer of 2011, something was brewing in the American consciousness that Laurie didn't understand, not then. Most people in California couldn't point to Yemen on a map, but they felt more solidarity with the disenfranchised there, with the revolutionaries in Egypt and Oman and Syria, than they did with their red-state neighbors. Over there, people had overthrown their oppressive rulers, demanded a better, freer world even if it meant civil war, and they'd done it with the technology built right here in Silicon Valley. At home, Twitter was used to navel-gaze and humble-brag about sex lives, while the rest of the world was using it for Democracy and Discourse, leaving them behind.

Maybe that was why Laurie finally sought out Ariel, and joined the tattooed and pierced ranks of Bridges & Borders, a San Francisco and West Oakland Workers' Collective focused on labor rights.

At first they loved her, called her their lost lesbian lamb ("It's okay if you don't use the L-word, most of us identify as queer or pansexual"). But over time they started to ask more of her than she was ready to give.

"Ariel said you're an artist. Can you design the T-shirts for our Pride float next year?"

"Can you spare five dollars a month for—

—my Kickstarter to support a BIPOC-owned yoga studio?"

—my GoFundMe for my top-surgery?"

—my Paypal so I can pay for my mother's cancer treatment?"

It was overwhelming, the misery of the American working-class, when she herself was barely making ends meet. What made her feel worse was the knowledge that if she fell through the floor financially, Mal would pick her up without a word.

Something started to change between her and Ariel. The air became charged, sharper. Ariel was the only one Laurie had told about Sophia, and earlier she'd been patient with Laurie's unwillingness to identify as *gay*, but now she was as uncompromising as Tara.

"Nick's a dick, but if you haven't told him, you're complicit in upholding the patriarchy."

"It was in the past."

"Not everyone has the privilege of passing," Ariel said. "How can you expect community when you can't do authenticity?"

Authenticity was all the rage, and the price of entry into society was divulging all secrets, demanding that people cut themselves open to bleed in the public eye. No more closets to hide in, no more private breakdowns in a therapist's office, no confessionals at AA. Failure was public, and so was redemption—with social media as judge, jury and executioner.

Years ago, when she fell (was pushed) into the pool at the Darling's holiday party, digital photographs weren't a thing. Now, instead of giving her a towel, people would be standing with their phones taking pictures to share along with a stream of emojis. It felt as if the time to come out privately was gone—life had to be *performed*, not lived. She was no longer a person but an instance of whiteness, of womanhood, of whatever was being scrutinized today.

The Darling no longer was one, and by working there Laurie was now the One Percent, even on her admin salary. She used to wear Darling-branded t-shirts; she didn't anymore. There were protests on the doorsteps of executives' mansions, stones thrown through windows of the leather-seated buses that plumbed through the East Bay. She stopped introducing herself as an admin when one of Ariel's friends called her a corporate parasite. It was no use telling them that she had bunions on her toes from forcing them into shoes too small for them for years. Just as it was no use arguing with Tara that she shouldn't have shared Mal's secrets with her as if they were a matter of common knowledge.

"Shall we ask Auntie Mal if she cares that I told you?" Tara demanded, chin jutting out defiantly. "You're projecting internalized homophobia and personal hangups. Honestly, the two of you are ridiculous. You could start a wildfire with all the pining."

"Mal doesn't pine."

She looked interested. "But you do?"

"I've got a date," Laurie said, and left the house.

She was off-balance. The ground was shifting underneath her feet in ways she couldn't predict. In the past this meant preparing for disaster—for a night-time escape from an alcoholic father, for a lie or a layoff to leave her staring at the rubble of her life. She sensed it in the way the women at Ariel's mixer turned their noses up at the scrawled *Bisexual* on her name tag, the way they smiled only with one side of their mouths when she mentioned she was currently dating a man. It left her wondering what would have happened if she'd stayed on the East Coast, with the old families and crumbling bedrock that had disavowed her. Or, more appropriately, that had renounced her mother as soon as her choices threatened them with upheaval.

California had history too, but it was cataclysmic, transformation after transformation changing the landscape beyond recognition. And yet, everyone accepted the weekly shifts of the tech industry and the San Andreas fault as a matter of course, they went to Napa and Healdsburg for wine that tasted like blackberries and black pepper and the ash of burning wind, and despite the Republican legislation that barred their way with the same frequency as the mudslides on the Pacific Coastal Highway, they held on to impossible ideals, like marriage, or labor rights, or bookstores.

Laurie loved California, but she didn't know how much longer she'd survive it.

• • •

In August, Mal invited her to come along to Ithaca, to drop Tara off for her freshman year at Cornell—though *invited* was hardly the word for what she actually did, which was to look up from her laptop and ask Laurie perfunctorily if she was buying two plane tickets or three.

Tara snickered in the corner.

Laurie glared.

"What? I'm playing Farmville."

"What about your parents?" Laurie asked, feeling petty, small, and tired. "They'll want to be the ones to see you off."

"That's a good idea," Mal said to her niece. "There's no need to start off your new life on bad terms, especially when there's precious little they can do to you now. Maybe they'll even pack up your stuff, so you have more than three sets of clothes. I can invite them here the night before we leave."

"Fine," Tara said, her face scrunched in an epic pout.

As they shopped and packed for Tara and prepared for the dinner, Laurie was hit by a sense of déjà vu. The last time she'd gone to the East Coast was for Christmas, when her mother was still married to Jim, her second husband. He'd picked her up from the bus-station in the leather-seated Odyssey he'd just bought, happy to show off the seat-warming feature. Laurie didn't know what he wanted her acknowledgement for more: the car, the marriage, or picking her up from the station.

"I've made your favorite," Mom said. "Chicken parm."

"Mom, I told you, I'm vegetarian now." She was dating Cam at the time, and had altered her tastes to suit his.

"I know! That's why there's no meat."

"Chicken is meat, mom."

"You shouldn't have to be vegetarian when you're on vacation," Mom said, turning away to hide her hurt.

On Christmas Eve, more people showed up, Jim's divorced brother and his two shy boys who stared at Laurie as if she were an exotic animal, despite her shapeless sweats.

"Can't you wear something nicer?" Mom asked.

"I don't like people looking at me."

"I want you to play something for us. So if you won't dress for me, do it for Brahms."

Laurie stomped off, dragooned into the role of the sophisticated city-girl who elevated Mom's social standing. She knew the score, knew Mom wanted to make Jim feel awe at having snagged someone like her, so he'd never smell the financial desperation that had been behind her agreeing to marry him.

She played the piano, even if the keys felt sodden with lake-effect snow, even though the audience of men—her two brothers, Jim and his brother, and the two shy boys—yawned through it.

"Good," Mom said, her disappointment soaking into that single syllable. She could make that word sound like such an insult, to convey the kind of solid, dependable and monetized mediocrity of a Starbucks or a Chrysler. Laurie had never left America, hadn't wandered through Vienna as she had, or walked through the Louvre, hadn't understood the way she strained towards transcendence and fell, each time, like Icarus with burnt wings.

Ashamed, Laurie disappeared into the study, while Mom went into the kitchen to finish cooking. She spotted a photograph there, of a much younger Jim, standing beside a woman in a sailboat. The woman was broad-shouldered, with tanned skin and large breasts that spilled luxuriously out of a skin-color bikini and denim shorts.

"That's my late wife, Eleanor," Jim said, startling her by entering the study. "Has your mom told you about her?"

She shook her head.

"You know, you kids, you wade into the water holding your hearts up high and dry. You get splashed and run screaming. That's not loving."

It infuriated her, that he was telling her this with her mother in the next room. But there was no point starting an argument when she was going to be trapped with them for the next three days, when Jim was going to give Micah a referral so he could get a job despite his prison record. So she just watched, helpless, as the men walked away from the table, leaving her and her mother to clean up. As, later, the men took up all the chairs, and Mom sat on the floor by Jim's knee and started to knit, functional and silent as a prosthesis.

• • •

The night before Tara left for college, Aditi and her husband Mahesh arrived just before seven, and their recriminations arrived shortly after.

"You should have told me Tara was here" quickly became "But how can I expect you to understand a mother's anxiety?"

And the knives weren't just out for Mal. "Tara, you're making Laurie and Mal take off from work?"

"She's not *making* us do anything," Mal said.

"No, she's shown she's perfectly capable alone, hasn't she?" Aditi said, one eyebrow up.

"I'm right here, Mom."

"Fine then, be on your own. It's not as if everything your father has done was to secure your freedom. So you can go to any school you want without worrying about paying for it."

Laurie felt too tense to eat. She too wanted to snap at Tara for being ungrateful, with her old acceptance to Carleton aching like a bumped bruise. But she said nothing, seated at the dinner table, an outsider in her own home.

Mahesh inquired after Mal's work at the Darling, neatly loading his plate one item at a time.

"Same as always." There was an edge to Mal's voice. Why became clear a moment later.

"You've been there nearly a year? Shouldn't you have been promoted by now?"

Laurie deployed herself to the kitchen to get a glass of water.

"People who can't deal with the working hours shouldn't be in tech," Mahesh was saying when she came back. "You can't expect to live some European lifestyle and still be paid Silicon Valley wages."

"Entitlement," Aditi added, nodding. "That's the thing. They all expect to get rich doing nothing. Retire early. What's that thing you told me about?"

"Instagram," Mahesh said.

"Right. A woman at my job left to post photos of herself doing yoga. She writes quasi-spiritual things, talks about *chakras* and butchers Sanskrit recitations and offers her services as a life coach. Who'd want to be coached by someone like that?"

"Just because you had to work eighty-hour weeks doesn't mean everyone else needs to suffer," Tara said.

"It's about integrity," Aditi said. "We owe it to ourselves and to those who came before to fulfill our potential." Her eyes fell on Mal with open disdain. "To do our best, not fritter away our gifts."

"And when is this debt paid?" Mal asked. "When we've made enough money? Climbed enough corporate ladders? Or had enough children to silence others' expectations?"

"To act on selfish desires when you know the pain they'll cause others is the height of irresponsibility," Aditi said.

The two sisters glared at each other, clearly having a conversation about something else entirely.

"What's this really about?" Mahesh asked, seeming to come to the same conclusion.

"Nothing," both sisters said at the same time, and turned back to their meals.

Eventually, when neither Aditi nor Mahesh made a move to leave, Tara walked over to the door, picked up their shoes, and brought them back to the hall.

"I need to sleep before my flight tomorrow."

"This—this isn't right," Aditi said, tears filling her eyes. "I don't know what ideas Mal's been filling your head with, but—"

"Go home, mom," Tara said, but kindly. "I'll call you as soon as the plane lands."

Laurie went into her room to give them some privacy. She heard the sound of feet going down the stairs. The air-mattress inflating in the hall. Dishes clinking in the kitchen.

Mal knocked on her door. Came in looking pensive, her curls tumbling out of a lazy knot at the base of her neck. "Thanks for staying through dinner," she said. "I know it can't have been comfortable, but without you as a buffer it would have been a much worse disaster."

"Any time."

"You don't *have* to come to Ithaca if you don't want to. It's a lot to ask, and I just realized I didn't really. Ask."

"I haven't seen my mom in ages, so I can get out of your hair if necessary."

"Actually you're the only person in the world I can stand sometimes."

Mal sometimes said these things—big, heavy, lifetime-memory things—as if they were entirely obvious. A few days ago she'd bailed on a fancy dinner with her colleagues to have pizza with Laurie instead, because the group of Stanford and MIT graduates was "too dull to be trapped with for a five-course conversation."

Laurie didn't want to seem nosy, asking about the rift between Mal and her family. But she got the sense Mal wanted her to ask, even needed to talk to her about it—something about how control and neglect were two sides of the same coin. Maybe they were stunted in similar ways.

"It's strange," she said, "how our lives seem to be twisted funhouse mirrors of each other. We're both the youngest of three, who've lost our fathers. Our siblings—"

"—were more like parents, and they resent us because they had to grow up too fast," Mal said, nodding. "The weight of it. I see it on them. It's what keeps my anger in check, that they've had to work harder."

Laurie got up and walked to her window sill, where she kept the crystals and rocks she'd collected over the years in California. From Haight-Ashbury's patchouli-scented shops with their little old white ladies in dreadlocks; from Esalen's sulfurous springs; from Bolinas, where they'd stopped on that road trip with Tara. She loved the agates most of all, their blossoms of lilac and turquoise saying that you could still be delicate even when you were strong.

"Salvador Dali loved agates," she said, picking up her favorite. "They look fanciful and free, but they're formed by unrelenting pressure." She pressed it into Mal's palm, closed her fingers around it. "It takes strength to hold on to joy when the world would rather see you broken and unhappy."

"Laurie…"

"Goodnight, Mal," she said, and closed the door. She didn't want to hear Mal refuse the gift.

You gave a millionaire a rock sounded in her ear so loudly she almost missed the way Mal said "Goodnight," softly, after her.

chapter ten

They left SFO early, tipped a wing in acknowledgement to the Golden Gate, and hovered for a while over the soft downy hills of wine country before leaving California entirely. Laurie had the window seat, and a panoramic view of the endless trucker towns with their desolate motels and dried-up pools.

"I can't believe you're actually reading that trash," Tara muttered to Mal, who was engrossed in some airport novel.

"I can't take snobbery seriously from someone who dreamed of getting married at the Cheesecake Factory," Mal said, without looking up from her book.

Tara scowled, and her knees resumed their nervous fidgeting.

"You can like what you like," Laurie said. "You don't have to justify it to anyone."

"I know that," Tara said.

Laurie waited. The truth would come out eventually. With Tara, it always did.

"My parents want me to major in Economics, but it's so boring."

"What do you want to study?"

"Economics would be good prep for Harvard's JD-MBA. It's a joint-degree program in law and business."

She raised her eyebrow. Tara hadn't answered her question.

"I like Cognitive Science, but—"

Mal wasn't saying anything, but her head was turned slightly, so Laurie knew she was listening. She was exceedingly careful with Tara, as if worried she might shape her too much in her own image.

"Don't you have a year to choose a major?" Laurie asked. "Why not just explore in the meantime? People tend to excel when they find their passion. It's always better to lean into your strengths than try to fix your weaknesses."

As soon as she said it she felt silly, hypocritical. Then again, if girls of Tara's generation could make their choices out of desire rather than necessity, the arc of the universe was bending towards justice after all.

They lounged at a restaurant in DTW on their layover, with Mal offering Tara a thimbleful of champagne to celebrate her independence responsibly. Laurie turned her phone off airplane mode to check her messages and found a *screed* from Nick.

Her stomach sank.

"Now, you'll likely drink in college," Mal said, "but never drink alone. And find a friend who'll keep you grounded, someone who makes sure you get home every night, that you don't send long emails to your exes or puke all over yourself in public. Laurie's saved me from myself more times than I can count."

It was her cue to share some funny story about Mal making a fool of herself, but Laurie missed it, being too overwhelmed to speak. She'd told Nick about this trip as soon as Mal booked it, and he'd never said anything. But while they flew from

San Francisco to Detroit, he'd apparently been composing a *long* email.

• • •

It's not that you keep running off with Mal that's the issue, but that you didn't even feel that you needed to ask me first if I'd made any plans that might be disrupted. I'm aware of how I'm coming across, like some 50s husband demanding a full account of your whereabouts. But if we don't have the kind of relationship where we make decisions together, are we even in a relationship? I waited to send this until I knew you would have time to think away from me. I'll ask again when you get back—what am I to you? No need to respond now, and email is likely the worst way to DTR. Just let me know what you want when you get back.

• • •

It went on for a few more paragraphs, apologizing for raising the issue and reaffirming his love for her. Guilt made her skin cool with sweat.

She looked up, hoping for reprieve or distraction. She couldn't think about this right now. At the next table, a harried mother said over and over, as if needing to play whack-a-mole with each of three kids, "I *said* no more Coke. I said *no*. You know what? You're done."

"Who charges four bucks for a Coke?" the father said, looking at the bill. "I'm not leaving a tip."

"Laurie?"

"Hm?"

"Tara was asking where you worked while you were at Cornell."

At Cornell glossed over the reality in a way she couldn't take right now. She wanted to snap at the family at the other table, to tell them that if they couldn't afford to tip they should stick to McDonald's.

"I worked in the diner," she said. "It was the only place that would take almost anyone, and I only had a high school diploma. The free meals were a big help."

Tara's eyes widened, but she said nothing.

They had to catch a connecting flight to Ithaca. Mal paid the bill and each took turns watching the luggage while the others went to the bathroom. In the stall, Laurie pulled open Nick's message and read it again. Unpleasant shivers went through her arms. Between the contents of the email and the cross-country flight she was constipated, and she flushed simply to reassure anyone waiting outside that she had a valid reason to sit in a stall for five minutes.

"All right?" Mal asked.

"Yeah," she said.

On the smaller plane going to Ithaca, she and Mal sat together, while Tara had her own row in the back.

"Oh, there's something I wanted to show you before we need to turn off our phones," Mal said. She showed her the website for a literary magazine, with her name listed as author.

"Mal! This is incredible!"

"My first publication under my own name," Mal said, drumming on her knees with excitement, "and you're the first to see it."

Laurie threw her arms around Mal's shoulders as best she could over the plane seat armrest. "I knew it would happen eventually."

"Well, I didn't," Mal said. "Anyway, I'll let you read it."

Laurie read the short story, recognizing it immediately as a twist on Oscar Wilde's *An Ideal Husband*. There it was a morally inflexible Lady Chiltern who could not abide her husband having the slightest flaw, as their marriage was based in her idealization of him. Here, it was an uncompromising Indian woman who could not stand the shame of her husband leaving a high-profile job for a more relaxed one. But he'd done it to spend more time with his family, when he realized his perpetual sore throat was in fact terminal throat cancer.

She reached over the arm-rest to hold Mal's hand tight. She didn't have to ask if it was autobiographical. Mal kept her face turned to the window, but her fingers tightened around hers.

"Please turn all electronic devices to airplane mode, and stow your tray tables for takeoff."

She finished the last of the story and put her phone away, but didn't let go of Mal's hand. The rumble of the plane reverberated through their clasped palms, and as they left the ground she felt a slight squeeze. The barest hint of nervousness. Somehow the thought that Mal, who flew around the world four times a year, who sauntered through security in her pocketless yoga pants after hitting world-records for unpacking her things into plastic trays, could still be nervous about flying, about her reaction to the story, about anything at all, tugged at a protectiveness she'd buried for years out of self-preservation.

She wasn't about to cuddle Mal and feed her soup, but she didn't let go of her hand until they were over Lake Erie.

• • •

As the small plane lurched towards the tiny Ithaca airport, Laurie itched to read Nick's email again, to torture herself with it. Her hand tingled with the memory of holding Mal's, as if singed by betrayal.

Mal procured and drove the rental car. Laurie adjusted to the shock of seasons. Fallen leaves blew across the windshield like harbingers. She'd forgotten what it was like to feel time pass, without being caught up in trying to save it or hold it back or convert it to other timezones to schedule meetings for executives. Forgotten what it was like to feel change in the bones instead of trying to make it happen on a screen.

They moved Tara into Dickson Hall. Laurie felt the stares of the other parents trying to make sense of their trio and tried not to squirm at the ghost sensation between her shoulder blades. Ithaca was a tiny blue star in an otherwise red sky. It was easy to forget that twenty miles out in any direction were conversion camps and conspiracy theories. It shouldn't have bothered her but it did, the thought that Jack or one of the people who used to know them might still work here and recognize her and think—

—So what if they did? What would be worse to them, Mal's race or her gender? Or would it be neither of these, but the ultimate betrayal of town versus gown? She could almost hear Jack growling, *You think a brown Barbie ain't a Barbie?*

The tension in the air crispened as they approached their hotel. She'd let Mal make all the plans, so she didn't know that they'd be staying at the Statler, where bellboys came to take her luggage as if she hadn't been working in the kitchens not too long ago.

"Are you all right?" Mal asked. "You've been off lately."

"Overwhelmed, that's all."

Her face softened. "It is strange being back, isn't it?"

Settling into the hotel made Laurie feel better. Mal lived out of her suitcase, ready to leave at a moment's notice. Laurie always preferred to nest, to discover the amenities of each place they stayed at, and put her things away in the little drawers and cupboards. She tidied up after Mal, putting their shoes into the closet.

"You don't have to do that," Mal said.

She hadn't said what Vic would have—*you're my admin, not my wife*—but Laurie's nose curled anyway. It was automatic, cleaning up the physical world when her mental world was a mess. Her first real date had been with the fry cook at the Cornell diner. He took her to the mall for Buffalo chicken pizza. She'd really wanted to make it work, had started to sense the edges of her attraction to women and wanted to reassure herself that a more ordinary future was possible. But he didn't try to kiss her, and it terrified her. Crying, she shampooed her carpet until two in the morning.

There weren't carpets for such catharsis in San Francisco. There were apps for door-to-door laundry service, for food delivery. Nick's studio was minimalist; if they fought she'd have nowhere to blow off steam.

"I remember thinking the Statler was so grand when I was a student," Mal said. "Now, it just feels a bit old and musty."

It was still grand to Laurie. None of the luxury hotels she'd booked for either the Unicorn or the Darling came close to having any history or character. Then again, she'd never have picked something truly beautiful for several hundred drunk guys to stay in.

"I think it's lovely," she said, then added, so Mal wouldn't think she was ungrateful, "Thank you for bringing me here."

"No prob. Shall we go for a drive before dinner?"

There was something about Mal at the wheel that felt safe, and every adventure they'd ever had only strengthened that belief. Once, in the early days of living together, they'd been on the 101 doing 80 mph in the carpool lane, when Laurie heard a loud *Bang!* and the car jumped and thudded.

"What was that?" she screamed, clutching the handle above her window.

Mal looked at her side mirror and frowned. "Hm... looks like the tire burst. Can you do me a favor and look out to your side into my blindspot? I need to get off the freeway."

Laurie did as told, not knowing what it meant to have a tire burst, telling herself that if Mal was so calm it probably wasn't so bad.

"Nice job," Mal said soothingly, as they crossed two lanes. "Just a little more to go."

In a daze, Laurie pointed out to her when it was safe to move lanes, and Mal took the exit and pulled the car over. Only then did Laurie see that the tire had blown out entirely, and shreds of rubber trailed the smoking rims.

"I was worried," Mal said calmly, "because the rims were sparking and they could've started a fire."

Laurie crouched in the grass with her head between her knees while Mal phoned Zipcar and let them know where they were. Even that wasn't enough to stop Mal short though—they'd abandoned the Zipcar to the company's GPS locator and continued onward in a taxi.

She didn't know her feelings for Mal then, but remembered noting the contrast between Mal and Cam when under pressure—Cam had entered a full-blown anxiety attack when a bike knocked the mirror on his parked car askew.

They drove up 89 towards Taughannock Falls. Laurie

stretched her arm out of the open window as if to touch the shimmering lake to her right.

"You're a million miles away," Mal said.

She shook her head. It was a frivolous thought, and not one she wanted to share with a published Writer. But Mal was looking at her expectantly, so she said, "It's strange that women are the primary readers of romance novels, but the books have the same structure as the male orgasm."

Mal blinked, once, then threw her head back and laughed so hard the car swerved.

Laurie yelped.

Mal stopped laughing, wiped her eyes, then started again. "I couldn't agree with you more. Maybe that's why I've never liked romance. Or weddings. How does it make sense to invest all your energy and money into one climactic moment? Where's the ROI in that?"

"You never even dreamed of getting married? Not even as a child?"

Clouds rolled in on her happiness.

"Weddings in my family are unpleasant," Mal said. "Everyone remotely related feels they can impose their opinion. Was the match appropriate? Was the event grand enough? Were the right dignitaries given due respect? Heaven forbid you didn't know your father's third cousin is a professor at the London School of Economics, or that somebody's grandmother was a princess before the old kingdoms united."

"Sounds... like a lot."

"It's a colonial scab. First they pick at it, then they go to make new cuts on fresh generations. All they need is the slightest reason, whether it's that you went to a lesser Ivy, or had an unconventional marriage—by which I mean marrying an Indian from a different *state*, not something truly absurd like marrying a divorcee or someone from another caste."

Her playful sarcasm did nothing to soothe or smooth Laurie's way. All she could think was, *Her family will never accept me.*

"Hold on," Mal said, and pulled the car over into a driveway. They rolled up to a butter-yellow cottage at the top of a small rise, surrounded by an acre of lawn and wildflowers.

Laurie stepped out of the car and saw the *For Sale* sign. She was about to say they ought to book a viewing, call the number on the sign, but Mal had already walked up to the front porch to knock on the door.

The lady who invited them in had short, white hair in a neat bob. Pockmarked hands quavered on a hand-carved cane.

"We're really sorry to bother you," Laurie added to soften Mal's request to see the house.

"No, no trouble at all," she said cheerfully, and let them in. "I like visitors. The real estate agent says the clients don't like having the owner hovering, makes them feel pressured. But me, I want to know who's going to have my house."

They stepped into a large room with enormous, floor-to-ceiling windows overlooking Cayuga lake.

Mal gasped. "This is stunning!"

The lady chuckled, pleased. "Yes, I know French windows are all the rage these days, but when I saw these in Venice I couldn't help myself."

"What do you think, Lo?"

"I could paint for hours with light like this."

Mal asked questions about the insulation and the roofing, while Laurie stared out at the lawn, wondering what she was planning. They got back in the car and continued driving, stopping at overlooks and parks along the way.

"Such a beautiful house," Mal sighed, as they crossed it again on the way back. "Three bedrooms, for a tenth of the cost of a smaller place in San Francisco. And close enough to the university that I could sublet it."

"And far enough away from everything else," Laurie pointed out. "Your job, the A.C.T., the ocean..."

Me.

"I can work over VC from anywhere. Well, it's something to think about."

Mal parked the car in the garage and they walked towards the Ithaca Commons. Again, Laurie became aware of how little she'd thought about the details of this trip, as Mal led them to *Just a Taste*, a restaurant so expensive she'd walked past it a hundred times. Her feet stopped at the entrance, like a horse shy of a puddle.

"Tara will be eating at the university," Mal said, as if that was what she might be worried about.

Laurie stared at the menu, her eyes scanning the prices. When the waiter approached, Mal ordered a flight of white wine for her and a flight of red for herself.

"I'd love to taste some of your whites too, if that's all right," Mal said.

She didn't usually seek any special permission about the finer points of ordering or sharing restaurant meals, so Laurie had to wonder if they had doubled back, suddenly, to a time when she used to pay her own way. The thought left her unsettled, on the edge of panic, and she turned to look out the window, where leaves scattered as if blown by an impatient breath.

When the wines arrived but she still hadn't chosen anything, Mal said, "I'll order a few things to share and we can go from there."

Laurie nodded, heartened. Their financial arrangements were one thing when they were roommates. But there was something about this trip, maybe that they were dropping off Tara like surrogate parents, or sleeping next to each other without a wall between them, or something that Nick's email had forced into the open—Laurie could see too clearly now what that relationship was not, and a sense of what she and Mal *were* was beginning to form, like an impressionist painting finally coming into focus with some distance.

The bill arrived and Mal placed her card in the folder and closed it decisively.

"Thank you," Laurie said.

"Stop thanking me for things."

As they drove up the steep hill on Buffalo Street, back to the Statler, Mal said, "I want to walk around campus tomorrow. See old haunts, help Tara settle in."

It wasn't an invitation, but with Mal this was often the closest it came to being one. It was always *I'm thinking of driving to Muir Woods; want to join?* all the way back to ordering a pizza in a hotel in Tahoe and knowing that it wouldn't go to waste. A pragmatic generosity, not a romantic gesture. Then again, why should love require impractical compromises, sacrifice… Laurie shook her head. She needed to slow down, back up to take in the whole scene. Nothing was clear to her; the dew collecting on the windshield seemed a sign.

"Can I borrow the car while you walk?" she asked. "I'd like to see my mother."

"Of course. If you're free in the afternoon, we can go for a hike in the gorge. It would be a shame to have come all this way and *not* do that."

Laurie banged her head slightly against the head of the car

seat. She *should* be planning to see her mother all day, and now she knew she wasn't going to.

• • •

As she drove alongside the rusty train-tracks, Laurie braced for the confrontations she knew were coming. Cayuga Lake looked so foreboding on the Lansing side, near the salt mines that ran for miles underneath the bedrock.

She pulled over into the driveway, wincing at all the things that hadn't changed since she'd been here so many years ago. The broken wheelbarrow tipped over onto its side, the chipping paint, the coffee stains on the porch, all signs of a house unloved brought into sharper relief by the memory of the Palladian windows on the house for sale they'd seen yesterday, on the more hospitable side of the lake.

Her mother opened the door and let her in, and she managed to keep her face expressionless despite the stale smell. She hugged her, noticing that she'd settled into the same squat, rural obesity as the GMO soy on the hills. They sat down at the dining table.

"Luke's at work, but Micah's out back." Mom sat down with a worrying groan, and her small hands trembled visibly. Her arthritis was worse. She probably couldn't play the piano anymore.

"How's Luke?"

Mom shrugged, as if there wasn't much difference between husbands when it came down to it. Maybe there wasn't. She'd never quite told Laurie what went wrong with Jim, or how she'd managed to keep the house in the divorce. Maybe Laurie didn't really want to know.

"How's Nick?"

Of course, Mom would ask after him first. Laurie had forgotten how glad she was when she told her they were dating, as if she'd been wandering in the forest and had found her way back to civilization. She needed to set expectations. "I don't think he'll ever pop the question."

"Do you want him to?"

She looked up at her mother in surprise.

"Take it from someone who's been married three times. It's rather overrated."

"And yet you always seem to find people ready to ask."

"Men of my generation tend to view marriage as a status symbol," Mom said. "It makes them feel respectable. Doesn't do much for the woman."

"Financial security," Laurie pointed out.

"That matters less than who sticks around to push you when you're in a wheelchair."

She blinked. Why was Mom talking like this? She was the one who'd once told her, "Never shop at Walmart, never let anyone see you there. The day you believe you're *poor*, you're done. People think poverty is infectious."

A door slammed shut, and Laurie turned to see her eldest brother. Micah had lost his hair, and the scar he'd acquired in prison gave him the look of a villain in a mob movie. He scraped the dirt off his boots and nodded at her.

"Hey, chiclet. Remember me?"

No biggie, he'd only tried to take her savings to invest in a scheme to steal people's social security funds, and then called her from jail after he was caught selling weed to university students.

"Hey, Micah."

He gave a loud guffaw, flashing yellowed, rotting, leaning teeth. A chill went through Laurie. He'd moved from marijuana to meth.

"It's been a wild few years," he said. "Jim defaulted on the house in the 2008 crash. The bank foreclosed, but they couldn't find a buyer because the house is shit. Covered in lead paint. I bought it for peanuts."

Laurie's jaw dropped. All these years, while she'd been watching *Breaking Bad*, she'd taken away intellectual insights from Walt White, and her brother had taken away a shoddy plan of action.

And now he had a house, while she didn't.

She stayed a little longer, but it was as if a great chasm had come between her brother and her. Her mother used to be the bridge between siblings, but somewhere down the line she'd made a choice, and let Laurie go.

It stung.

She got up to leave. Mom got up with another groan to see her out, and Micah headed out back. She didn't want to stay to find out what he did there.

"You shouldn't judge your brother too harshly," Mom said. "We all make the best choices we can."

"I'm worried."

"People usually are, when they see other people doing things they wouldn't do."

Laurie frowned. She thought she might be trying to tell her something important, trying to connect past the chasm.

Mom's voice trembled. "You will visit again? And not let so many years go by?"

"I want to," Laurie said. It was the truest thing she could say.

"Not if it's a hardship," Mom said. "The last thing I want

to do is to drag you down."

"You don't."

She looked away.

Heartsick, Laurie drove back to meet Mal on North Campus, where she was saying her goodbyes to Tara. The teenager surprised Laurie with a hug, whispering in her ear, "She's an oblivious idiot. You're going to have to spell it out for her."

Laurie didn't bother denying she knew what Tara meant, just glared in warning.

She and Mal climbed down the trail into the Fall Creek gorge, pausing at the outlooks to catch their breath.

"She's going to be okay," Mal said. "Tara, I mean. The whole truth of the matter finally came out. She was dating some guy back in California, who dumped her when she got in to her top schools but he didn't."

"What an ass," Laurie said.

Mal shrugged. "It happened to me too, a few times. Sharing my salary was the easiest way to weasel out of arranged marriages."

Laurie snickered. She could see the affront on those placid and self-assured faces when they found out the truth. When Mal first joined the Unicorn, so many people had started off with some version of "*Who does the new girl think she is?*" and come back a few months later as devotees, prefacing every sentence with "*Mal says*" as if she were some minor deity. Laurie couldn't imagine what it must be like to be a man raised around the identity of being a provider and husband, only to meet someone like Mal and discover that those services were no longer necessary.

"Is it common to just share your salaries outright?" she asked, closing her eyes for a moment to take in the familiar *silisilisili* of the flowing creek below. "When does it come up, the second date?"

"They're more like interviews than dates, but it's usually a first date sort of thing. Some people even put it in their online bios. Why?"

"Salaries change. Seems like a stupid thing to veto a marriage over."

"People don't *have* to get married."

"No, but they do have to pay rent."

Mal frowned, as if she couldn't understand how the two things were related.

They continued climbing, reaching an area where the river was shallow enough that they could walk through it. Behind them was the loud hiss of a steep waterfall, a precipice of about thirty feet. Ahead was a smaller waterfall, only five or six feet, over which the water fell softly as a curtain, smooth and translucent. They walked over to the side, where they could hang on to the overhanging rock of the cliff for support as they climbed. Laurie went first, her callused palms gripping easily onto the shale as she stretched for the next foothold. She reached up and launched herself over the last few feet. She stood at the top, grinning, and turned to offer Mal her hand for the final ledge.

She hadn't imagined that Mal would be looking at her instead of finding her next foothold.

One moment she caught sight of an awed smile that made her chest expand three sizes, then the next, Mal's hand slipped, and she fell eight feet down the small waterfall, landing in the shallow river with a sickening crunch among the stones.

No.

For a long moment, Laurie stood in stunned silence.

The river, though shallow, was strong, and the current began to pull Mal down towards the steeper part of the incline. Laurie screamed, and Mal seemed to hear it because she started to grab for something, anything, to avoid being pulled farther down over the precipice of the steeper waterfall.

"Hold on, I'm coming!"

Laurie climbed down the way she'd come up, working to slow and measure her movements, knowing that if she went down too, they could both be killed. Her hands shook. Flakes of shale slid off the cliff. Was Mal holding onto something? Had she already fallen over the lower edge? Would she have heard a scream over the roar of the waterfall? She didn't dare look. If she did, she'd lose time and possibly her balance.

She stepped into the river, crouching low and keeping her eyes only on Mal, who was holding onto a large rock with her left arm to keep from being dragged further downstream. The water was deeper than it looked, and it rooster-tailed up over her torso and thigh as it bore down and past her. Laurie reached for her freer arm. Both their hands were wet, slippery, and it took a couple of agonizing tries before Mal caught her wrist and she hers.

Laurie pulled with everything she had, until Mal's feet found purchase against the rock and weren't hanging off into the air. Mal got to her feet, stumbling, and Laurie dragged her to the side of the river, to where they'd left the trail.

They sat down heavily. Blood flowed down Mal's legs, and there was an endless array of cuts down her knees and shins. More stains started to bloom on her shirt and against her khaki shorts.

Laurie's vision felt super-saturated, as if she was seeing high into the ultraviolet.

"I need to see if anything's broken, okay?"

"It doesn't hurt."

"That can be bad. Shock comes first, pain later."

Laurie was crying, sobbing openly even as she spoke what she knew were facts.

Mal reached over to cup her face. "Come here." She pulled her into a hug.

"I was so scared. I thought you were going to die," Laurie said.

"I'm here," Mal said, and kissed the side of her head. "I'm here."

Laurie pulled away abruptly, adrenaline still coursing through her, making her actions stuttering, erratic. She didn't trust herself not to shatter into a million pieces.

"Lift up your shirt," she said, rubbing her arm across her nose to clear away the snot. "I need to see if you broke any bones."

Mal winced as she did, but there didn't seem to be any restriction of movement. Laurie ran her hands over the cuts on her ribs. They bled freely but they weren't too deep.

"You're okay."

"That's what I said."

Laurie didn't stop crying. Something in her had shaken loose, and she couldn't stand the thought of being separated from Mal, even for a second. She reached for her hand, and Mal let her hold on tight.

"Thank you," Mal said softly.

"Shut up. If I can't thank you for dinner, you can't thank me for this."

Laurie felt rather than heard her laugh, the vibrations doing more to calm her than all her careful breathing. With difficulty, she got up and they started walking back up the trail. From time to time, she'd have to let go of Mal's hand to climb a particularly difficult part of the path, but they both reached for each other as soon as the trail widened into flat, soft, mulch.

Once they were back on campus, heading towards the Statler, fear drained slowly away and embarrassment seeped into the spaces it left. They were dripping wet, bras showing through now-transparent shirts. University students turned to gawk. Mal simply walked into the Statler, bleeding knees and all.

A group of housekeeping staff stood near their room. Their joined hands broke apart like legos.

"Can I have some bandaids sent up, please?" Mal asked.

The staff scurried to accommodate, and Laurie couldn't help but remember the waiter in the taqueria falling over himself to fetch her a chair.

What did it take to walk through the world as Mal did, a free intelligence, a sovereign nation unto herself?

Mal rinsed off quickly in the shower while Laurie opened the door to accept the box of bandaids. Mal sat on the bed in her bathrobe, revealing her legs to be bandaged. Laurie wouldn't let her apply the bandages, but cried again as she did so herself.

"Please don't cry," Mal said. "I mean, this was just Darwinism at work. My soft, useless hands didn't have enough calluses to hold onto anything properly."

"*Don't*," Laurie said, suddenly furious. "Don't *do* that."

To Mal's credit, she understood. "I'm sorry. I've trained myself to put my feelings aside when they're inconvenient."

"Well, don't do it with me," Laurie said, more sharply than she'd ever spoken to her. "Don't *ever* do it with me."

"Okay," Mal whispered. "I promise. I was scared too... I must have been. But I don't know how to let myself feel certain things anymore."

Laurie was flooded with sudden, overwhelming pity. She

buried her face in Mal's lap and put her arms around her waist, and cried the tears Mal couldn't.

• • •

She was still shaken the next day, and flying back without Tara meant no distractions. Laurie ached to lift the armrest and feel Mal's shoulder against hers. Instead she composed replies to Nick's long email in her head, wondering whether and how to reassure him.

They landed at SFO and got an Uber. Mal threw her carry-on into the trunk and got inside, and was already fiddling with her phone by the time Laurie got in.

"Huh," she said. Looked up at Laurie in wonderment. "I got the house."

For a moment Laurie drew a blank, then it all hit her at once, like a rushed backstory montage in an indie movie. The drive up to Taughannock. The Palladian windows. But buying a house ought to be an ordeal, a matter of weeks of planning and thought, like having a baby. It wasn't… you couldn't just…

Apparently Mal could. She could buy a hundred-and-fifty-thousand dollar house with cash, on an impulse, in less than forty-eight hours.

"Wow," Laurie said lamely, trying to muster up some enthusiasm.

Mal leaned back, grinning with satisfaction. "Well, that was a successful trip."

Laurie fell silent, turning to the window. In the rear view mirror, her face had the sallow, dead-eyed stare of a Modigliani.

As always, the feeling came first. Cracking the window to let in the chilly autumn air did nothing to help. She doubled over and put her head between her knees, stiffening when Mal's hand landed on her back to soothe.

Mal asked if she was all right. She'd been asking that a lot. The answer didn't come to Laurie until they entered the city, when they pulled their suitcases out of the trunk and climbed the stairs together. Then she heard the words from Nick's email in her head.

If we don't have the kind of relationship where we make decisions together, are we even in a relationship?

She stared at the back of Mal's head. *We're not in a relationship. I've just acted as if we are.*

Humiliation. That's what it was. A feeling so far beyond embarrassment that she'd skipped over burning cheeks and flaming ears and landed on hollow devastation. She wanted to lock herself in her room, to delete all her social media accounts, to move to a new state. Anything that could erase this lie of a life she'd lived, believing them to be more than roommates, friends.

Was it her fault? What had Mal been thinking, flying her to Hawaii and Ithaca as if they were on a honeymoon, providing her with champagne and romantic six-course meals at every turn?

Maybe—horror froze her limbs—maybe Mal was indulging her so she wouldn't kick her out of the rent-controlled apartment. Maybe Mal knew her feelings perfectly well, and had been serving them well enough, but keeping her at arm's length so she could save up for that cottage she'd just bought.

Making her believe she had a chance, when she was going to leave all along.

She picked up her phone and wrote to Nick.

If I asked Mal to move out, would you move in with me?

He'd probably be angry with her for not responding to his email right away. Or sore that when he'd asked her to move in with him, she'd said no. Or—

Yes.

Laurie stared at the message.

Before she could lose her nerve, she got up and walked over to Mal's room and knocked on the door.

Mal let her in and resumed unpacking her suitcase. When Laurie didn't say anything, she stopped and turned to face her.

"There's something I have to tell you."

Relief broke out over Mal's features, lit golden by the setting sun. She gave her a warm smile. "Are you going to share whatever's been eating at you this whole trip?"

Laurie nodded. She folded her arms to hide their nervous twitching.

"Nick wants to move in with me."

Mal smiled widely. "Laurie! Congratulations! That's such a huge step!"

Tara was right. She really did need things spelled out.

"But that means you'll have to move out."

"Sure," Mal said. Her smile didn't slip for a second. "Were you afraid I'd be angry or something? Of course, I understand. Will the end of the month be soon enough?"

Laurie couldn't speak without saying something she'd regret, so she nodded and left the room, but not before she saw Mal return to her unpacking, as if nothing had happened.

chapter eleven

In September 2011, once Nick and Laurie had settled in and made a few trips to Bed, Bath & Beyond, Laurie returned to Bridges and Borders to reconnect with Ariel.

Ariel wasn't happy to see her. "It's been a while. How was your vacation from the horrors of our lives?"

"Don't be like that. I was helping Mal with a family situation."

"Is she your family then?" Ariel asked, and swept her arms around her. "Because that's what *we* are. A family. Not some means of redeeming your white guilt when you're not gallivanting with your rich pseudo-girlfriend."

"Mal's moved out," Laurie said. "I want to help."

Ariel shrugged and walked away to set up the tents, leaving Laurie to help with putting together signs, preparing the troops for their planned protest. A petite androgyne with waist-length dreads and a nose ring worked at Laurie's desk.

"Do you suppose something will come of all this?" Laurie asked, in an attempt to make conversation.

"What do you think we should do then? Write letters to our reps, wait patiently for Obama to care about the working class?"

"He doesn't?"

"Of course not," the androgyne said, scoffing. "Doesn't seem to matter to *your* people that he's kept the war going, or that he's bailing out banks while Lozano raises college tuition fees to the point where none of us will ever own a house or be more than indentured labor."

"Who's Lozano?" she asked, more to avoid the part of the sentence about *your people*. Whichever people it was, it couldn't be good news.

"What the hell are you doing here when you haven't even bothered to educate yourself on the problem? Lozano's on the Board for the University of California system. Next thing you'll say you've never heard of Ward Connerly either."

She shook her head.

"Well, let's just say, you can't fix systemic problems with dark faces in high places."

She was thrown back to how Cam had once called an acquaintance "very Franzen" and then apologized for making a reference she wasn't expected to know. Being berated for not being fluent was still better than being pitied for not being conversant.

"I'm Laurie," she said.

They looked at her skeptically. "Ayo. They, them. But seriously, what are you even doing here?"

"Ayo!" someone called, and they skipped away without waiting for her answer.

Laurie focused on the sign she was making. *People, not Profits.* Not since Cornell had she felt like such an imposter. What *was* she doing here, trying to assert her solidarity with their ideals while she lived with a rich techie in her rent-controlled apartment?

She told Ariel she didn't think she was helping.

Ariel nodded sagely. "Let's unpack that. Why do you think *helping* is what we need from you?"

Laurie sensed the anger behind the question. *Helping* was right up there with *Raising Awareness* on a website cataloguing stuff white people did. "What else then?"

"Lo, look around you. We're not an *organization*. We're a *community*. If people don't accept you as you are—if just *being* isn't enough—those aren't your people. If you think you need to *do* something to belong, you're trapped in the very capitalist system that only values people for the output they deliver."

Mal had been telling her this all along, but for some reason it only hit her now, like a wave of exhaustion cutting every synapse at once.

"So what do I do?"

"Go home. Find yourself. Then your people will find you."

She did, heart bruised. For the rest of the day, she was lost in thought. For some reason, Will's words from years ago kept repeating in her mind. *Finding yourself is getting more and more expensive.*

She asked Mal to meet her for brunch. Since Nick had moved in, the two of them went to work together, and he didn't understand the point of making a detour to Bluebottle when the Darling gave them all free breakfast and coffee. So Laurie hadn't seen Mal in nearly five weeks. Surely enough time to be rid of any uncomfortable situational sexual feelings, which is what she hoped they had been.

Mal asked to meet at Foreign Cinema on Mission Street. *No fun going there without you.* Nick raised his eyebrows but said nothing. To him, fancy restaurants were for special occasions, not Saturdays. Laurie didn't know if he made more money than Mal or less, but Dolores now came to clean only every two weeks, and the ice-cream in the fridge was Häagen-Dazs, not Bi-Rite.

"You've spoiled me rotten," she said to Mal, as they sat down at a corner table.

A waiter smiled at Mal in recognition and asked, "The usual to start?"

"For her too," she said, then turned to Laurie. "What do you mean?"

Laurie started laughing. "Mal, one of the fanciest restaurants in the city knows you so well they're going to bring out mocha, champagne and lavender-flavored goat cheese. You do realize nobody else lives like this? For the rest of us, San Pellegrino is luxury."

Mal smiled half-heartedly, and Laurie felt guilty. She hadn't meant to shame her, hadn't really thought Mal was capable of feeling the sting of someone else's words.

"I wanted to ask you something," she said, changing the subject. "Are you in touch with Will at all?"

"No, why?"

"I was just wondering what drew you to him."

Mal didn't answer for a while, and their waiter brought them their beverages. Laurie covered the baby blue Acme coffee cup with both her palms, enjoying the perfect warmth.

"I suppose it was that he was unapologetically himself," Mal said eventually. "Most people are too caught up in the stories of who they're trying to be, you can practically hear their self-conscious thoughts as static noise. Does my belly show in this dress? Do they like me? Do I sound interesting? What if I fart during sex? He was…" She smiled. "Quiet. It helped my mind quiet too."

"How do you think he got that way?"

"He claims it was magic mushrooms."

Laurie stared, and Mal laughed.

"Something about breaking down the pretensions and boundaries of the mind. Apparently he spent a summer picking vegetables with migrants, wandering through fields of knobby artichokes and endless strawberries. He met someone there who introduced him to peyote and psilocybin."

Somehow, the idea of Will working as a farmhand refused to resolve into an image in Laurie's mind. In all the time she'd known him, despite his mountain-biking and rock-climbing, he'd always seemed so urban, even literary.

"Well, yes," Mal said when she mentioned it, "That was why he did it. Following in the footsteps of a generation of mangsty dicklit. Every guy goes through a pseudo-Buddhist phase, trying to walk away from the world when he finally realizes he's not in control of it. It's just a more intellectual way of abdicating responsibility."

"I thought you admired him."

"I *envied* him. I suppose there's always some envy involved in attraction. You never really know if you want to just be with someone or to actually *be* them."

They ordered their main courses, and Laurie sipped on her champagne and marveled at the idea of Mal envying Will for his summer of white guilt. There was no doubt in her mind that was what it was. She'd seen so many others like him, over the years, who left high-paying jobs to install solar panels, or build orphanages, or help the Obama administration modernize. They helped rebuild New Orleans in the wake of Hurricane Katrina, but always returned to some suburban home with IKEA furniture. To a wife and kids.

"There's a tradition in Indian weddings I've always hated," Mal said. "At some point during the wedding, the groom has second thoughts. He's not ready to settle down. He wants to go to Kasi, to gain knowledge and become a saint. But the bride's family begs him to come back and gives him gifts so he'll marry their daughter." She added quickly, "It's all in jest, of course. These days, people just say whatever the priest tells them to, they don't understand any of it."

"No wonder you never want to get married."

Laurie hoped she didn't sound as bitter as she felt. And that was exactly the kind of thought Mal had just said created static noise.

"I wanted to ask you something too," Mal said. "At work, did people ever treat you differently because you're a woman?"

"Did they ever *not*?" Laurie said, then realized she was serious. "Mal, every day is Russian Roulette. Guys are either asking me out or asking me to bring them coffee, and the girls are worse, talking about how awful it is that someone mistook them for an admin."

"I didn't realize," Mal said, frowning. "They've never really done that with me."

Laurie blinked. There was oblivious and there was whatever defense mechanism blinded people to uncomfortable truths that were entirely obvious to everyone else. When they met, Mal had revealed Laurie to herself in a taqueria. Maybe it was appropriate they come full-circle here, at one of San Francisco's finest restaurants.

"Mal, how many other women are on your team?"
She frowned.

"*You're* the real unicorn," Laurie said. "They don't treat you as a woman at all—but that's because you don't act like one."

"It's strange," Mal said, looking thoughtful. "My boss keeps asking me to talk to other women about how I've leaned in, broken ceilings, cleared paths, as if I'm some kind of rabid construction worker."

"He wants you to enforce the patriarchy."

Mal's eyes widened. "That's sick."

"You've never worn a skirt to work."

They were quiet for a while. Laurie wondered if she'd gone too far.

"We spent so much energy trying to play a rigged game," Mal said eventually. "This generation just won't play it anymore."

"True," Laurie said, thinking of Ariel and Ayo. "They might question their gender but not their right to unionize. We have more to learn from them."

"Exactly," Mal said, face clearing. "Thanks."

When Mal paid for brunch, Laurie tried not to think about whether she had been sufficiently entertaining as a companion to deserve it. To free herself of the transactional worldview that capitalism had successfully infected her with before she even knew what a transaction was.

Instead of going straight back home, she went to the Embarcadero, where Ariel and the others had set up their *Occupy SF* tents on Justin Herman Plaza. The strangeness of the colorful tents and unkempt crowds against the backdrop of bizarrely tidy and symmetrical palm trees left her profoundly disquieted. There was something dishonest about the constructed urbanity of San Francisco, about the delicate pastel hues of the buildings that lined its streets. There was always more truth in the alleys, in the voluptuous naked women painted on the walls and the shit-stink of politicians who were fighting the move to create free automatic public toilets.

Thirty dollars per flush, they complained from their million-dollar homes.

There was a commotion at the intersection. Laurie walked over automatically, her steps quickening at the sight of flashing blue lights. Two cops, together over four hundred pounds, towered over Ayo, while Ariel had her camera out.

"Why do you need to see my ID?" Ayo shouted. "Are you arresting me?"

"Sir, you could be arrested if you don't comply."

"Don't fucking call me *Sir*. My pronouns are they, them."

"Is that what it says on your ID?"

Heart pounding, Laurie stepped forward, tucking a lock of hair behind her ear. Years of watching Mal at meetings should have prepared her—but the hulk of metal at the cops' waists, the glint of their buttons and badges, the blue menacing lights—meetings with techies rarely ended in violence.

But she was in too deep. "What's going on, officer?"

"Please don't interfere, Ma'am. We'll have this cleared right up."

"I could help," Laurie offered. She mentioned—*casually*—who she worked for at the Darling. "I could call him up and ask if he wants to issue a trespassing charge or if he's cool with leaving them alone."

She couldn't, not really. But she opened her purse just wide enough for him to see her badge.

The cops retreated.

Ariel gave her a look of grudging appreciation. "Maybe you *can* help."

It was only later, after several hours of putting up posters and passing out bottles of water, when she arrived home with multicolor stains on fingers that smelled of Sharpies, that she realized what she'd done.

That Ariel had filmed the whole thing. Her arrogant bluff. If it was posted online, if her boss saw it, she could lose her job.

She trembled for hours but didn't regret it.

chapter twelve

That year, for Thanksgiving, Nick and Laurie invited home a few friends each, mostly from work. Mal didn't come, just sent them a note saying she'd be driving down to Montara to write.

"I guess I should be glad she didn't pack you along as her muse," Nick said, putting an arm around Laurie's waist.

He'd grown more affectionate, but also less passionate. It had been weeks since they'd done anything beyond giving each other a kiss before turning in for the night. They'd only gone back once to the pleasure coach, who recommended they join the group stroking event to learn from others, and that was a step further than Nick's pride or possessiveness would allow.

But Laurie wasn't going to let her anxieties rule her again as they had with Cam. She was going to host Thanksgiving dinner and sleep through the carb-coma afterwards.

She let the conversation wash over her, the usual work anecdotes and complaints peppered with unsolicited life advice.

"Have you tried—
—Bikram yoga?"
—an ironman?"

—cryotherapy?"

—floatation tanks?"

One couple had just bought a house in Oakland so neglected that they'd had to rent goats to make sense of their yard. Those who weren't improving their homes were improving themselves, with lessons in skydiving, machine learning, scuba diving.

Everyone seemed to be going somewhere, driving up and down the 101 for the smallest reason, flying to LA for Coachella, to Austin for South by SouthWest, to New York for lunch, devouring distance as if it were a glass of chardonnay.

Leaving her behind.

Talk went to the new VP hired in to oversee the organization.

"He seems nice enough, but I was explaining config deployments and you know what he asked me? What's a server? *What's a server!*"

"What do you expect? I saw on LinkedIn he went to community college, back in the *eighties*. What's next, DeVry?"

They started laughing loudly. Nick gave her a concerned glance.

"Come now," she said, "the eighties had *some* redeeming qualities."

"Top Gun!"

"Thriller!"

"Pac-Man!"

"What about you, Laurie? What do you wish you could bring back about the eighties?"

"Oh, so many things," she sighed. "I mean, this generation will never know the feeling of unbearable anticipation that comes with the sound of a modem."

Everyone started laughing.

"Other things too," she said, glad to lead the crew out of choppy waters, "things I wish I could share with the next generation. Pointless but beautiful things, like mix-tapes, or cursive writing."

"Nick, you never said your girlfriend was a comedian."

"She's a riot," Nick said, but didn't sound pleased.

Later, as they cleaned up the dishes and wine-glasses, he said, "You ought to consider going back to college, maybe get your degree part-time."

It took everything she had not to hear that as an insult, but as a genuine desire for her well-being. Still, her voice wasn't entirely steady as she said, "I'm not sure I could spare the time, or the expense."

"It's an investment," Nick said. "I'm sure there are loans. You're so smart... once you have a degree you wouldn't have to stay an admin forever."

"I *like* being an admin," she said, knowing it was true as she heard it come out of her mouth. It was rather like being the conductor of an orchestra, soothing tempers and managing personalities so a team could function. Of knowing everyone's secrets, often before they knew themselves.

"How did you end up working with Vic?" Nick asked. "The man drops names like seagulls drop shit. Did you have to interview with him?"

She clenched her teeth. Nope, not an insult. Not an insinuation that she might have lied to Vic or slept with him to get the job.

"He hired me out of a bar," she said, passing Nick a scrubbed pot to dry. "He was trying to socialize with a group of guys to get them to invest, but they thought he was coming on to them. He just... didn't know how to engage. I took him aside, asked him a few questions, and then went to the guys to introduce him properly."

"And of course they listened to you because you were a pretty woman deigning to talk to them."

"That was part of it," she said, stilling the bloom of anger. "I just knew them better. They were regulars."

"Of course," Nick went on, obliviously. "You've always been good at getting your way. It's subtle, but now that I think about it, you can pretty much influence anyone to do what you want. For most engineers, that comes across as magic."

She braced against the sink.

"I prefer to think of it as empathy," she said. "It's not something you can get a degree in."

"Still, not everyone's going to give you a job based on your ability to manage a group of drunk guys. A degree is insurance."

"Why does it matter to you?"

"Oh, not to *me*," he said hastily. "But it does matter to other people. I just don't want anyone to turn their noses up at you."

And therefore at me, if I'm standing beside you.

She wiped her hands on the towel and went into the bedroom. She couldn't be angry with him, not when she would never consider taking him home to meet her mother or brothers. Her mind whirled, with *If people don't accept you as you are*, and *We spent so much energy trying to play a rigged game.*

When Nick had moved in, she'd let him have the entirety of the second bedroom for his home office, and part of her bedroom for his things. Now she had no refuge. Her room no longer felt like her own.

Nick fell asleep first, and she went out into the living room, glad to see Mal's chat status indicating she was still awake.

How's the writing going?

Productive. Nothing like a drive to clear my head.
Do you think I should go back to college and get a degree?
Why?
Do you think it would open doors for me?
What doors do you want opened?

Oh, the aggravating woman! How was Laurie to know what doors she wanted opened when she didn't know what doors were there in the first place?

I want

Her fingers stilled, unable to complete the sentence. Every time she tried, her thoughts drifted.

Mal had to be frustrated waiting for her, because she wrote back first.

Put differently, what do you wish you were doing with your time?

Well, that was easy enough. *I want to be learning something new.*

You always did need to be challenged.

For a long time there was no further response and Laurie thought the conversation was over, but then a bunch of links appeared, each leading to an art college admissions page or an evening program at the Academy of Art for adult education. She clamped down on her excitement, refusing to let herself fall in love with yet more things she couldn't have.

If any of these strike your fancy, I'd be happy to foot the bill.
Why? Why would she offer that?

She couldn't accept, but she couldn't bring her fingers to type fast enough to refuse. Mal had already added, *You can pay for the supplies.*

Laurie put the laptop away on the couch and stared at the fireplace. A course she could handle. It wasn't too much commitment, wasn't too expensive, and if it didn't work out she'd know early, instead of worrying about failing out of a university after a lengthy admissions process.

She messaged Mal back. *You're not just saying this because of what I said at brunch the other day?*

What did you say at brunch?

Never mind. If Mal didn't remember, she wasn't going to remind her. *Are you sure?*

I wouldn't offer if I wasn't. I never do anything I don't want to do.

Relief coursed through her. This, more than anything, Laurie knew to be true. Mal's lack of social graces freed her from the burden of expectation, of second-guessing. She understood, now, what Mal had meant about Will.

Mal's so-called selfishness was her salvation; it quieted her mind.

...

"Do lesbians like tongue rings?" Valentina asked, sticking her own tongue out experimentally.

Mortified, Laurie put her head down on the desk. Even so, she could feel the eyes of everyone in the classroom on her.

"What?" Valentina asked. "It's for a character I'm designing."

When she'd started the course in digital animation, Laurie had known she'd be older than most others there. She had *not* expected Valentina Garza. The girl was a potent mix of classical beauty with forest green hair, of insatiable curiosity and celestial ambition, and she'd made it her mission to turn their group into either a found family or a drunken bacchanal, or both. She couldn't tell.

Nobody had managed to hold themselves back from Valentina. *Nobody.* Within a day, they knew each other's Twitter and Instagram handles. Within a week, Valentina had everyone sharing their favorite kinks in their AO3 fan fiction. After their evening classes they headed out for drinks and sketching sessions, trading tips on layer manipulations and cheap Korean spas. Pretty soon even the fifty-five year-old divorcee was playing "Never have I ever," and confessing to kissing one of the Gallagher brothers from Oasis.

Many nights Laurie came home bursting with ideas and drew until one or two in the morning. A series of Matryoshka dolls, a matrilineal lineage that ended with her, who'd never have children. The California coast, a Gothic blur of watercolor greens and monstrous waves. Anything. Everything. Once she looked up from a sketch to discover it was three o' clock and her heart was racing.

Huh. I like drawing more than sex.

Such a strange thought! She started laughing, but it felt like a deeper truth she really ought to have known. Not wanting to second-guess herself, she sent the sketches to Mal with a *Sorry, still getting used to drawing on a tablet* before she went to sleep.

She was glad of Mal's *These are incredible!* but didn't think anything more of it, until Mal phoned her a week later and said she'd shared them with a friend of a friend who just happened to be a producer of an animation studio that was doing work for Netflix.

Laurie started hyperventilating.

"Don't worry, he loved your work. He wants you to do some character designs for him, and he'll pay a commission. Laurie? Why are you crying?"

There was opening a door and there was shoving you through it, and of course Mal didn't know the difference. Naturally, she'd never seen a door she didn't blast her way through.

"What if he doesn't like it?"

What if I fail and it reflects on you?

"You'll still get paid, and you'll learn from it for next time. Besides, if he likes it, who knows?"

Next time?!

Laurie was still a watery mess when Nick came home. He'd been working longer and longer hours in hopes of a promotion, and she was just a personal item on the shelf at this point. Got girlfriend? Check. He didn't even notice when she didn't come to bed but stayed up drawing furiously till dawn.

Never in her career had she worked so little and got so much done. As if her mind was now free to be creative in the off-hours, and could be clear and focused at work. She managed to save her Director's marriage by getting him home by six every day and hooking him up with an entire network of service professionals—tax accountant, financial advisor, clothes stylist, hair stylist, therapist and door-to-door laundry—to counter his workaholism. Most tech executives had never learned how to adult, and were surprised to discover that their wives didn't really want to mother them anymore. In his gratitude, her director surprised her with a promotion. She was finally making a living wage.

Naturally, she was terrified. There was nothing quite like success to cue all her instincts for self-sabotage.

Mal didn't understand her fear, but reluctantly agreed to stop paying for her art classes.

"It's something I need to do for myself," Laurie said. "So it feels more real."

"By the way, the producer liked your character designs. Everyone else is either too much in the Marvel style or too traditionally manga. You were able to surprise him."

"I could tell in the descriptions that he wanted something pre-Raphaelite, although he didn't know that was what he wanted."

Mal laughed. "You always know other people so much better than they know themselves."

Except you.

That evening, after art class, she noticed Valentina was quieter than usual. Laurie stayed by her side as they went out for drinks, and didn't have to wait long until the younger girl started talking.

"My parents got sent back to Mexico in August," she said. "And I would have gone with them, except in July…"

"The DREAM Act," Laurie guessed. Since the verbal thrashing from Ayo, she'd done her research. The legislation had only just passed in July, allowing minor children of illegal immigrants to study in California. "You got a scholarship."

Valentina didn't smile. Instead, she clutched at her heart. "Don't say it *so loud*."

Yeah, Laurie knew that terror well. The knowledge of the precipice behind your heels even as your hands found purchase up ahead.

"I've been thinking, maybe I shouldn't risk it. Even with the scholarship, I'll still have to take out a loan, and if I don't get a job…"

"You'll get a job," she said quietly. "It might not be the one you want, at least not at first, but you'll push through. A chance at the life you actually want is worth the risk."

Now, if only she could believe it herself.

"I always feel I'm going to screw it up somehow." Valentina crossed herself. "I put the sugar in the fridge, and couldn't find it for days. I don't know how to file for COBRA. I need to get a scooter or something to get to school, but those things are manual and the only clutch I know is a handbag."

"And maybe it would be easier if someone else made all the decisions? Do you really want that though?"

"How do you know you're not going to screw everything up?"

"Oh you will." Laurie laughed. "But at least you'll be the one doing it. Or at least that's what you'll tell yourself, each time you screw up. And I can help you with COBRA. I'm something of an expert."

Valentina leaned her head on Laurie's shoulder and sighed. "You're really awesome, Laurie, you know that? Like, you make me wish I were at least a little gay."

Laurie stiffened instinctively, then relaxed and laughed.

chapter thirteen

a few weeks before Christmas, while she was at work, Laurie got a call from Tara. For a second she didn't pick up, thinking she must have called by mistake.

"Tara?"

"Hi, I don't have much time. I called you because Auntie Mal never picks up her phone. I need a favor."

"Sure, what is it? Do you want me to get her?"

Tara gave a hollow laugh. "*Want* isn't the right word. But I don't suppose you have a thousand dollars to post bail, do you?"

Laurie grabbed a notebook and pen and started writing down details. "Which station are you at? What's the charge?" A distant feeling of shock registered, like the fading reverberation of walking into a door. She gritted her teeth.

Tara answered all her questions, and then said, in a shaky voice that reminded her she was still only a teenager, "Thanks, Laurie. You're really good at this."

"We'll be right there," she said. "California usually insists on two days of jail time for a DUI, but especially since you're under twenty-one, they might be willing to let it drop to a misdemeanor with community service."

After the call ended, she used their internal systems to ping Mal urgently and tell her to get out of whatever it was she was doing and grab her things. Mal responded only with *omw* and walked over to her desk.

"What is it?"

Laurie nodded towards the exit. No sense in talking about it in the office, where others might overhear. They left briskly and started walking towards Market. The BART would be the fastest way to the police station on Valencia.

"It's barely five o' clock!" Mal said when she filled her in. "Why was she even drinking at this hour, never mind driving?"

"Just don't yell at her. Trust me, she's scared and alone and has probably never seen the inside of a police station in her life."

"I'm not angry, just—"

"Disappointed?"

"Confused," Mal said, but looked as if Laurie had slapped her.

Never had she thought she'd be the steady one between them, nor that her time spent navigating the fallout of her brothers' bad decisions would turn into a skillset she'd ever use again. At the police station, Mal sat quietly with Tara in the processing room while Laurie filled out the paperwork and paid the cash. She and Mal had each drawn the daily limit of five hundred from an ATM to avoid the long line at the bank for a cashier's check.

"I'm so sorry," Tara said, sobbing so hard she could only wheeze out her words. "This is going to hurt your credit score."

"That's hardly important right now," Mal said.

"It would also only be true if we bought a bail bond on a credit card." Laurie kept her voice light. "I don't know who's been feeding you these myths, but maybe cut back on the HBO."

She tucked away the inventory search and tow receipt for

the car, and they headed out of the police station towards her apartment on autopilot, before she remembered Mal no longer lived there.

"Nick won't be home for a while?" Mal asked.

"Who's Nick?" Tara asked.

"My boyfriend. Remember? And no, he won't be home until at least nine."

Tara frowned at them, uncomprehending, but followed quietly.

"Your parents can pick you up here," Mal said. "I'll let them know where we are."

"Can't I stay with you?"

"Of course you can," Mal said, "but you're a minor, so you can't keep this from them. They're already driving up."

Tara fell silent, shuffling along silently. Laurie let them in and made some chamomile tea, served it alongside a scoop of vanilla ice-cream.

Mal mouthed a silent *thank you*.

"I wonder if they'll bring Grandma," Tara said softly. "She arrived last night for the holidays."

Mal's shoulders pinched together, but she said nothing.

They had, in fact, brought Mal's mother along, and she seemed to have cried the entire way here. Her eyes were so red she might have seemed drunk herself. Aditi was white-faced, and her husband Mahesh looked rabid.

"This is absurd!" he cried, stomping about the living room. "She's an Ivy-league student, not some thug. This is racism, that's all it is."

"It's probably a factor," Mal said. "The bottom line, though, fair or not, is that people like us aren't allowed any mistakes, and her BAC was 0.05."

Laurie winced, thinking of Micah and his meth dealings.

She'd never told Mal about that, or about her father's alcoholism, or about having family that strained not just the wallet but the very limits of love. It made her sad sometimes, and envious of the way everyone in Mal's family assumed, even when they were fighting, that they would still be given food and a bed and more love than they maybe wanted at the time. Tara could just show up on Mal's doorstep, certain of her welcome. Laurie hadn't wanted to mention how her mother had waited to know she would be staying at the Statler before saying she'd be glad of a visit.

"What were you thinking?" Aditi asked Tara. "What were you even doing up here?"

"Aditi," Mal warned.

"It was a brunch party," Tara said, "with all my high school friends. They're living in Berkeley now."

"Berkeley... You're telling me you drove drunk *over the bridge*?"

"Aditi, the bridge isn't the issue here," Mahesh said. "What kind of friends are these? I'd like to have a conversation with their parents."

"To intimidate them, you mean," Tara said, eyes blazing. "As you've done all my life. I'm lucky they still talk to me."

"What are you talking about?"

Tara stood up, incensed. "Let's see. I suppose you didn't consider it condescending to go on at graduation about how the UC system isn't competitive because they guarantee acceptance to the top ten percent of students."

"Well, it isn't."

"What about when you told Mediha's dad that you wouldn't pay more than a million for a house in San Jose, because the neighborhood wasn't safe?"

"What was wrong with that?"

"Dad! Mediha's mother is Afro-Latina! She *is* the neighborhood! You want to talk racism, let's start there!"

"Are you saying this is somehow *my* fault? You decide to drink to show your useless friends, who'll never go anywhere, that you're one of them? You're not!"

Laurie slipped away to the kitchen. She wasn't family. It wasn't her place to hear this. But she wasn't fast or far enough to miss what came next.

"This is clearly Malini's influence," said the grandmother, who'd been crying silently this entire time. "She and her friend introduced Tara to this lifestyle."

"What *lifestyle*?" Mal asked, her voice a knife.

"You know perfectly well. You're just like your father. Selfish. You don't care who you hurt."

For a long moment, there was silence.

"Get out," Mal said.

"*Excuse* me?" her mother said.

"This isn't your house. It's not even mine. Tara, you're welcome to stay with me as long as you like."

"She's a child!" Aditi said. "Clearly she's incapable of making good decisions on her own."

"And who are you to her anyway?" Mahesh added. "We're her parents, and she isn't even eighteen."

"Are you going to drag her out of here physically?" Mal asked.

"What are you doing?" her mother asked, panicked.

Frightened, Laurie rushed into the room to see Mal holding up her phone camera with the little red square indicating she was recording.

"Waiting," Mal said calmly, "for you to leave my friend's house."

"This is—"

"Tara, you'd better—"

"I'd better *what*, Dad?"

They were all protesting at once, but they squirmed away from the camera's view, picking up their jackets, putting on their shoes.

All except Tara.

Within moments they were gone. Mal put her phone away with a bitter laugh. "They're more afraid of being mocked on Twitter than of being audited by the IRS." She dropped her hands to her sides and gave Laurie a look of apology. "We'll be leaving too."

Tara's eyes were on Laurie, pleading and lost. She swallowed visibly.

"Tara?"

"I… I forgot you weren't living together anymore."

Mal frowned, not understanding. But Laurie did.

"Did you want me to come over too?" She turned to Mal. "I don't know if you have enough room for me to stay over, but—"

"If Tara takes the futon, and you're willing to share with me…"

"I'll pack my bag." It would have to be all right.

Within minutes they were in an Uber, heading over to Mal's apartment in SoMa. It was strange to be driving sedately down Folsom Street like some sort of family, when the last time Laurie was here, three years ago, her coworkers were at the Folsom Street fair being spanked by drag Jesus or whipped by a leather-clad Nefertiti. But already the dive bars and warehouses were being replaced with skyscrapers and apartment complexes, and the men who wandered around Mint Plaza waving genitals and manuscripts and signs warning of the apocalypse had been replaced by people like them—women in LuluLemon who refused the heterosexual American dream and chased down their morning-after pills with brut rosé.

San Francisco was growing up, and she was glad of it.

They ordered Indian food and packed Tara off to bed before she could ask questions about why Mal had so many spare toothbrushes. Then they went into Mal's bedroom and stared at each other blankly.

"It's silly, but I really want a glass of wine."

"Me too, honestly. Do you have any?"

Mal nodded, but didn't move.

"It feels wrong. After what happened."

"Ah," Laurie said. "I bet Tara's fast asleep after the day she's had. You could easily get some from the kitchen without waking her."

Mal stayed put.

"Mal, this wasn't your fault. Since when do you feel responsible for other people's choices?"

"I gave her that first taste of champagne, remember?"

It was a long moment before Laurie did, before that frazzled layover in DTW even registered in her mind. "Mal, two celebratory sips of champagne at an airport doesn't make you an alcoholic. I'd know."

They slipped quietly into the kitchen, careful not to wake Tara. Mal grabbed a bottle and they returned to the bedroom with two empty glasses and a corkscrew.

Mal opened the bottle slowly, quietly. She sat on the bed and drew her knees to her chest, looking suddenly small and vulnerable. "There's something you said earlier. It's been bothering me."

Laurie's heart sank. "It's been a stressful day. If I offended you—"

Mal shook her head. "Far from it. You reminded me of something. Even before my dad died, my mother was… well, the usual story. Came to America terrified and overwhelmed and entirely unprepared, and nothing we did was ever good enough. When my father got promoted, she pointed out that in India he'd be a CEO whereas here he'd always be less than his white counterparts. And when he quit it all to teach…"

Laurie sat down on the corner of the bed diagonally opposite her. For a long time, they just sipped their wine in silence.

"Even before he died, Ashwin and Aditi were always harping on me for some reason or another. I wasn't focused enough at school, I didn't do enough of the housework, I embarrassed them in front of their friends. I was a *lot* more awkward than I am now, if you can imagine that. We didn't have words like neurodivergent back then, and god forbid someone were to call me that. To make us seem anything other than perfect."

"I can't say I know what that was like," Laurie said, when Mal looked at her expectantly, "but I do know what it's like to feel you're always letting people down."

"Maybe that was what started it," Mal said, looking away. "I found something that helped me manage the stress of it. I don't know how it occurred to me, I certainly hadn't read up on the internet about the neuroses of high-functioning teens, but I found that if I had an X-acto knife and an hour to myself, I could handle anything afterwards."

It took everything Laurie had to keep from reacting.

"You can say what you think," Mal said, pouring herself a second glass. "It's plain to see on your face. My father looked at me the same way when he caught me. It was the first and last time he ever raised his voice."

Laurie downed the rest of her wine and held out her glass

for a refill. She was already slurring; she didn't have Mal's robust tolerance, and just then she didn't want it, either. Not when the way the wine gushed out of the bottle was so like—

"What did he say?"

"I was a bit of a smartass. I said, *Let me guess. You're not angry, you're disappointed.*"

"Oh."

"He shook his head. Said, *No, I'm FURIOUS. You hurt someone I love. I don't know how to forgive that.*"

Tears started rolling down Mal's cheeks. Laurie stared in aghast fascination. In all these years, she'd never seen her cry. Mal wiped away the tears with her hand and looked at her wet fingers in surprise.

"Huh," she said. "I didn't think I *could* cry. I haven't, you know. Not in forever. Not even when he died."

"Mal, that's…"

"Not normal?"

"Not *healthy.*"

"I couldn't. Everyone was falling apart, so I arranged everything. The funeral, having the body sent back to India so it could be cremated properly. Ashwin and Aditi were already married, living on opposite sides of the country. I had yet to go to college, so I had to get my mother where she needed to be. She was terrified, and so angry—"

"Angry?"

"You heard what she said. She thought he was selfish. He could've gotten a few more months with chemo, and left us a lot more if he'd stayed in his original job until the end. I guess she never really understood him."

"But you did."

Mal sipped her wine and leaned her head back against the

headboard. Her dark eyes softened; took on a faraway look. "I asked him about it. It didn't make sense to me, and I could see my mother was upset, so I went up to his bed—he couldn't leave it anymore—and asked, *Why didn't you choose to live a little longer?*"

Laurie gasped.

Mal smiled. "Yeah, I was a *lot* more direct back then. I've since learned that most people don't appreciate it. But he did. Maybe it was because I was genuinely curious as to the answer. I wasn't judging; I just didn't understand. He couldn't really speak anymore, so he typed out the answer. It was just three lines, but they changed my whole world."

"What were they?"

"Law of diminishing returns. Living isn't enough. Joy is a necessity."

"Mal," Laurie said slowly, "he wasn't saying that you didn't have a right to grief. Or that he was leaving because you were bringing him diminishing returns."

"I know that," she said, without meeting her eyes.

"Do you? It sounds to me like you believed he left to protect his own happiness, but he quit his job to spend time with you because *you* were his joy."

Mal frowned.

"I've known people who've had chemo," Laurie pressed on, knowing she had to cauterize the wound. "If the cancer is terminal, and all it brings you is a few months, that too a few months when you're bedridden with pain and unable to speak or eat and a burden to everyone around you, it's not worth it. He wanted to live as long as he could live *joyfully*."

Mal's fingers loosened around her wine glass, and it teetered dangerously. Laurie reached for it before it could fall, but Mal flinched and the wine spilled onto the floor. Neither of them even glanced once at the spill. Laurie placed their glasses on the nightstand and grabbed Mal's hands in hers.

"I know how terrifying it is to believe," she whispered, not daring to pull away, "that you might be worth loving just as you are. How could you feel that if someone hadn't shown you?"

Mal blinked, and tears slid down her cheeks. Laurie couldn't bear the refusal in her eyes, the sheer, shocking uncertainty. She pulled her close and down to the sheets, letting Mal cry into her shoulder.

She'd never remember what she said, what she whispered in her tipsy haze, but they fell asleep like that, in each others arms.

At some point in the middle of the night, Laurie woke up needing to pee. Mal's eyes were open, tracking her as she got up. She didn't know whether Mal had been awake long before her, or whether they'd woken together. When she came back to bed, Mal's hand stretched out towards her, hesitant to go back to where it had been resting on her hip. Laurie reached for it and threaded her fingers through Mal's. Mal shuffled closer. She did too. Soon their heads were on the same pillow.

Mal moved first, settling in so close their noses touched. Her warm breath landed against Laurie's lips.

Mal's hand returned to her waist.

Laurie lifted her hand to Mal's cheek.

Their lips met. Hands started to explore, to pull and tug until their legs intertwined. It was so easy. Comfort and love and grief came unbound. They kissed until Laurie's lips were bruised, and didn't stop, and when Mal pressed her into the sheets her legs wrapped around Mal's hips as if they'd always belonged there.

chapter fourteen

They startled awake at the knock on the door. It was just as ridiculous as the movies, with the canned look at each other and the shared disbelief, and two disorganized bodies jumping out of bed in alarm.

Shit. Tara. Nick. What had they done?

Laurie rummaged through her things for her phone. Her heart sank at the dead screen. What time was it? At least it was a Saturday, so she wasn't missing work, but she'd meant to tell Nick she was staying over at Mal's and hadn't.

"Charger?" Mal handed her the wire's end. Rubbed her neck awkwardly. "You always did forget."

Laurie gestured towards the blossoming red mark there in the shape of her lips. "Do you have something to cover that?"

Mal's eyes widened, and she tossed two piles of shirts to the floor in her search for a scarf or a turtleneck.

"Third hanger from the left," Laurie said, recognizing the glimpse of plum-colored wool. She set her phone to charge and looked around for a mirror. Of course there wasn't one.

She opened the door a fraction and said to Tara, "We'll be right out."

"Okay," Tara said. "It's... um, noon. I'm getting kind of hungry."

Mal went out first, and if Tara wondered why she was wearing a sweater over her pajamas, she didn't ask.

Laurie checked fervently in the bathroom mirror for any traces of last night. Finding none gave her no relief. She turned on her phone, taking note of the nineteen missed calls from Nick, and the anxious messages from everyone including her boss.

She called Nick first, rambling an apology that made her cringe. He was silent.

"Nick?"

"This isn't working."

It was her turn to fall quiet, waiting at the edge of the bed.

"I'll move out at the end of the month."

"That's next week," she said.

"I'm sure Mal can foot next month's rent," he said bitterly. "It won't be long until she moves back in. I don't understand the two of you and I'm not sure I want to."

She didn't argue. She couldn't even think about last night without feeling dizzy and slightly nauseous. She didn't know what it meant, if Mal even remembered. She'd thought nothing of comforting her. Hadn't even remembered to feel guilt.

"I'm sorry," she said, biting at the stubs of schoolboy nails. "I wanted to make it work."

"I believe you believe that." He sighed. "I need to be with someone who doesn't take independence to the blackout level."

He was right. She'd never given him a chance, never told him about Sophia, or anything that mattered about herself. She'd willed this relationship into being, driven hard by a flinty, unrelenting pragmatism.

"I'm sorry," she said again.

"I'll see you later," he said. "I've got to start packing."

For a long time after the call ended she stared blankly at the wall. Eventually Mal knocked at the door.

"Aren't you hungry? Lunch is here."

She wasn't hungry, but she ate in a daze, unable to follow the conversation between Mal and Tara. She snapped back when someone called her name, urgently, as if they'd been calling for a while.

"Are you all right?" Tara asked.

"Just hungover."

Then she realized what she'd said. Mal looked guiltily at Tara, who hung her own head over her pizza.

"I guess I owe you an explanation," Tara said.

A sharp twinge went through the space between Laurie's shoulder blades. This was too much like the climactic reconciliation that came at the end of an episode of Full House—super-saturated colors, flawless skin and gentle tones—and she'd never been able to watch a single episode without hearing her parents fighting as background noise. It made the quiet dignity of Tara's confession terrifying because there was no shouting. Yet. That was the thing about trauma—even when you knew this moment was not the same as what had come before, your mind had been trained to expect danger to follow signal.

Sounds hollowed out, became echoes. Past superimposed on present. One minute it was Micah, furious with her for not handing over her savings. "You're a child! What do you know of fiduciary management? Can you even spell fiduciary? I'm your brother! You don't trust me? Are you stupid?" Another moment and it was her mother, clapping a hand over her mouth, holding up a Minnie Mouse backpack and whispering, "Don't say a word. Just get your shoes on. We'll stop to pee."

Laurie's fingers clutched the tabletop. *Hold still. Avoid attention.*

"You don't *owe* us, but we'd love to understand," Mal said, her tone collected, as if she were solving a math problem.

They were sitting at the same table but they seemed so far away Laurie wondered if they saw her. Aunt and niece were having the Full House conversation while she was the invisible audience that laughed and said *Aww* in the right places.

"It's strange," Tara said. "All this time I was worried I was leaving them behind. My friends. That they'd resent me for going away, for choosing a private college, when really I'm the one who got left behind. They were so *real*, all of them, talking about things that mattered, *doing* things that matter, and I—I felt like a geek, some disembodied poser who'd never really lived or loved or done anything worth doing."

Don't faint. This isn't about you.

"It takes time for some of us," Mal said thoughtfully. "I used to think people were crazy, getting into bad relationships and worse breakups, backpacking across Europe and staying in sleazy places, destroying themselves as fast as they could with alcohol and drugs. If I tried to help, they got angry and called me a robot or a bitch or worse."

"What changed?"

Laurie didn't miss Mal's sidelong glance. Infinitesimal, but gratifying. Hopefully Mal couldn't tell she was on the verge of an anxiety attack.

"Writing helped," Mal said. "In fiction, my characters could feel the things I couldn't. I also took baby steps. Maybe I didn't feel like the protagonist yet, or even the villain or sidekick, but

I was a supporting player in the overall story, maybe even the glue, or what they call the fifth business in an opera."

A supporting player? Ha. A tornado masquerading as a breeze. Anger had the benefit of cutting through the fog a little.

"So you think I tried to jump straight to tortured protagonist?" Tara asked with a small smile.

"Sometimes you can't climb out of the ivory tower; you just have to fall. But it's less lonely out here."

Silence fell, but it wasn't uncomfortable. Silverware clinked against Mal's hideous egg-white Corelle bowls. Mal's priorities—sturdy and dishwasher-safe—had resurfaced as soon as they'd started living apart. Laurie found her feet, and they found the cold uninviting tiling of the SoMa new-build floor.

"What shall we do today?" Mal asked.

"I should call my parents," Tara said in a small voice. "To arrange a lawyer, and pick up the car, and whatever else."

Laurie brought out the tow receipt and other paperwork. "I should head home, but you know you can always call me, any time."

Mal called her an Uber and walked her out. She was quiet, but Laurie could tell she was thinking hard. She didn't interrupt to thank Mal for the Uber; it meant as little to Mal as the five dollars she left to tip room service at hotels. Perfunctory; the *noblesse oblige* of someone who had always had servants and paid for those servants' school and hospital bills.

Stopping mid-stride, Mal took a sharp breath in. "Last night—"

"Nick and I broke up this morning," Laurie said, before Mal could say they'd made a mistake.

"You told him?"

"No. It was mostly unrelated. I didn't need to hit him while he was down. He's moving out next week."

Mal nodded, then looked up, worried. "Do you need me to cover for next month's rent?"

"It's not your fault he's moving out."

Well, it was, but not because of last night.

"Do you want me to move back in? I don't want to presume, but if you need to find a roommate fast…"

Fast.

She'd floated from Cam to Sophia to Adam to Nick with an ocean of Mal all around her. She'd gone from treading water on her own to cruising along with the tech wave, buoyed constantly by Mal's gleaming generosity. Now here she was in sudden financial straits and Mal held out the lifeline that could draw her back to the comfort of a world she knew, one where she felt the relative stability of a surfboard at speed… at least until the next wipeout.

"No," she said. "I don't want that."

"Laurie? I'm not offering out of guilt. Just being practical here."

A sudden surge of orgasmic rage nearly lifted her off her feet.

"Mal," she said slowly, "I think you're talking logistics because you don't want to think about what we did."

Mal flinched, proving her right.

"Last night… wasn't an accident. Not for me. And I can't go back to us being just *roommates*."

"We were never *just* roommates."

"You bought a house in another state without telling me."

"What does the house have to do with anything?"

Laurie felt terribly hungover, exhausted and dangerous as a cornered animal. She finally said it all in one loud rush. "Were you living with me because my apartment is rent-controlled? Just so you could save up for it?"

Mal gaped. At least that was a relief. The thought hadn't even crossed her mind.

Tears stung Laurie's eyes. She needed to get out of there.

"Mal, I'm in love with you. I've *been* in love with you. But it doesn't matter, because, unlike you, I need to get married. To feel *safe*. And that's just not in the cards for us, for many reasons."

And she turned and walked away, towards the BART, speeding up as she went. She didn't look back even when Mal called to her.

chapter fifteen

After Nick left, Laurie went into that larger bedroom she'd rented out ever since she first came to San Francisco. She'd signed the place for those East-facing windows that let in what little there was of the city's sunlight, but she'd never lived there herself.

She ought to rent it out again, but she couldn't. Something in her resisted sharing that beautiful, sunlit room. A desperate need for space, maybe, or for clear edges around her.

She moved her easel and all her art supplies into the large room, converting it into an art studio. Why shouldn't she have this? With what the Darling paid her, she could cover the rent herself if she was careful, or she could rent out her own, smaller, room.

One month. Just one month to myself, then I'll see.

• • •

There was a message from Mal on her phone: *Can you give me a range? Are we talking weeks, months, or was that your polite way of saying never?*

Mal was still busy untangling Tara's situation, but she'd asked when they could talk, and Laurie had asked her to give her some time. She'd heard from the rumor mill at the office that Mal was doing well, that something had made her more focused than ever, and she was in line for another promotion. Only Laurie knew that meant Mal wasn't doing well at all. Sometimes, in the chat window they had open, she'd see Mal typing a message, the three dots dancing enticingly at the bottom for several minutes before going still.

Weeks, I think. Not years, she typed. *Definitely not never. Thank you. If you need anything, just ask.*

Same to you. Keep me posted about Tara.

A few days later, Laurie went to see her in juvenile court. Together, Mal and Laurie stood behind Tara, who trembled in front of the judge but bravely admitted her guilt and apologized.

"It was my first time drinking," Tara said, "and I didn't know I was drunk. I thought I was fine because I'd only had one glass. I didn't know that vodka was that strong. But I shouldn't have been drinking at all, and I shouldn't have been driving afterwards. I'm sorry, and it'll never happen again."

She accepted her sentence of four years of misdemeanor probation with a stoic nod, and insisted on paying the fine of one thousand five hundred dollars out of her own work-study earnings.

"Proud of you," Mal said.

Tara nodded, and her eyes flitted uncertainly to her mother. "Mom."

Aditi was ashen, as if she were committing a crime simply by being in a courtroom. She turned to the lawyer. "You said she'd get jail time."

"I needed to prepare you for it," he said. "Most kids get jail time. But most kids aren't as articulate or as obviously contrite as your daughter."

Aditi nodded, then convulsed into sobs, as she finally allowed relief to soften her.

"*Mom*!" Tara cried, embarrassed.

"Let's go home," Mal said.

Laurie nudged her and whispered, "Empathy, Mal. Empathy."

Mal looked at her and followed her gaze to Aditi. For a moment she looked confused, then she gave her sister an awkward hug. Aditi leaned into it gratefully.

"Okay, now let's go home."

"Can we eat something first?" Tara asked. "I haven't eaten all day, I was so nervous. I didn't want to throw up in front of the judge."

"Of course," Mal said. "My treat."

"Laurie, will you please join us?" Aditi asked, wiping her eyes.

Laurie was too surprised that the request was coming from her rather than from Mal or Tara to refuse it. They went to Dosa on Valencia, where they ordered comfort carbs in every variety, eating as if they hadn't for weeks.

"I wanted to apologize for my mother," Aditi said to Laurie. "For all of us."

"It was a stressful time for you," she said.

"I'd like to believe that who I was that day isn't who I am, not really," Aditi said, "but neither stress nor alcohol turns you into a different person. It just brings out the worst."

"Really, it's all right."

"No, it isn't," Aditi said. She blinked away tears and gestured at Tara. "I can't watch my daughter accept responsibility for her actions and not do the same myself. You're the one Tara called when she needed help. You earned her trust where I'd failed her."

Tara and Laurie both looked down at their plates. Laurie was glad of the interruption of the waiter asking about desserts.

"Mahesh…" Aditi swallowed. "It'll take him some time. He's too proud."

"He just can't stand having a juvenile delinquent for a daughter," Tara muttered.

Laurie must have looked confused, because Mal explained, "He's cutting Tara off."

"Don't worry about it," Aditi said, patting Tara's hand. "Our mother got cut off too, because hers was a love marriage at a time when that wasn't done. But as soon as Ashwin was born, she got welcomed back with open arms."

"Great, all I need to do to earn my father's supposedly unconditional love is to have a boy child?" Tara asked. "Amazing. Dad of the year."

They ordered dessert, found the few empty places left inside themselves to fill up with, and left the restaurant. Tara was still staying with Mal, so Aditi was going to spend some time there before heading home. Tara took Laurie aside for a few minutes and hugged her close.

"No matter what, you can always call me," Laurie said.

Tara gave her a knowing look. "Whatever's going on with you and my aunt, don't let her off the hook too easily. Sometimes she just needs to be told where to jump, and she'll take a leap of faith."

"What do you mean?"

"I mean, half the reason my mother's so mad at her is that she was always allowed to do homework rather than housework. Oh, brilliant, genius Mal, fluent in three languages, doing trigonometry since she was eight, she's too much in her own world to bother with us mere mortals. Why make her clean up her own messes or do her own laundry? I'm telling you, she *can* change. She's just never been asked to."

"You think I'm angry with her?"

"You kicked her out of the house, didn't you?"

"Tara!" Mal called. "Are you coming?"

"Just a minute!" Tara turned back to her, looking surprised. "Laurie, I live with her. She's a fucking mess. She thinks I don't notice when she's staring off into space looking like a kicked puppy. Whatever she did, you have to let her know so she can apologize."

Laurie was too stunned to answer, and Tara left to join her family. She wanted to talk to Ariel, but when she started to explain the situation over the phone, Ariel said, "Hold up. I'm not nearly sauced enough for this conversation, and besides, who talks over the phone these days? Get your ass in gear and meet me at The Café."

Laurie hesitated.

"Tell me you know The Café, and you didn't think I meant a coffee shop," Ariel groaned.

"I've been there before," she said archly.

"Have you now? I want *that* story first."

She wore the Armani Exchange sequined coral dress she'd found at the Buffalo Exchange for five dollars, and took the MUNI over to the Castro. At once the *thumpa thumpa* of the dance clubs and gyms reverberated around her, and the rainbow flags that had greeted her when she first got to San Francisco electrified and pumped her heart, boosting her courage if not her mood.

Ariel shuffled from one heeled foot to another at the entrance to The Café. She was wearing fake eyelashes that seemed to curve right up into her eyebrows and bright turquoise eye-shadow. In her iridescent dress she seemed almost like a mermaid. They climbed up the stairs to the dance floor. Within minutes they each had a gin and tonic and found a seat at the edge.

"So, you've been here before?"

"Yes, before the remodel."

"Ahh," Ariel said knowingly, sipping at her drink. Waiting for Laurie to say it. The Café had been taken over by gay men, but had started out as a lesbian club.

"Fine, I was here on a date with a woman."

Ariel smacked her lips, miraculously leaving their glittered shine intact. "Tell Ariel *everything*."

"It was mortifying. We met at Ritual, or rather she saw me at Ritual and asked me out and I was too shell-shocked to say no. I mean, I'd only been looking at her because she'd been looking at me, but she thought I was checking her out and—stop laughing!"

"You're such a disaster," Ariel said. "Go on."

"Anyway, she insisted on *driving* me here, and it's only a ten-minute drive, but we made it in six. She raced up and down the hills to make the timed lights. I was nearly sick by the time we got here, and I'm fairly sure the wheels left the ground once. Then she brought me here and ordered a whisky sour for me, even though I told her I can't stand the smell. It makes me sneeze."

Ariel shook her head. "If you wanted to date a man in a woman's body—"

"Yes! Exactly! That's what it was! Anyway, we drank and talked, just as you and I are doing now. Then she grabbed my hand and started pulling me towards the dance floor. I said I needed to pee first, and…"

Ariel waited expectantly, then her jaw dropped. "You panicked."

"I panicked."

"No, you didn't. Tell me you didn't just cut and run and then ghost her."

"I didn't stop running until I got to Tartine."

"*Laurie.*"

"I know," she sighed. "I *know*. I'm a terrible, awful person."

"You really are."

"I cheated on Nick, twice over if you consider not telling him about Sophia, and I'm the reason Mal's now spiraling out of control."

"Wow."

"I know."

"No, wow, as in, most people are wondering if they dare disturb the universe, and here you're convinced you're some sort of Casanova, wrecking people's lives willy-nilly, as if they're not grown-ass people making their own decisions."

Laurie looked up at her, confused.

"Let's dance," Ariel said. "Before you decide to pee again."

Laurie followed her to the dance floor, where go-go boys danced with their groins at eye-level, folded twenty-dollar bills lacing their thongs.

"I chose the wrong profession," Laurie said ruefully.

"Add that to your list of crimes."

"So what do I do?"

"What do you want from Mal? A declaration?"

She cringed. If Mal said she loved her, would she even believe it?

"What then?"

She tried to answer after another drink, when she was giggling over nothing and far too buzzed to care. Still, it didn't feel wholly right. "I want her to see me the way I see her. She's *so annoying*. Every day is a surprise. It's been five... no, six? At least five years. And I can't stop thinking about her. I want—"

"To annoy her just as much?" Ariel asked, smirking.

"Yes! Why can't I be annoying? I'm like a pillow." She flapped her hands, searching for the word. "If I'm not careful I get smashed by other people."

"Well, you're certainly smashed now. Let's get you home."

They stumbled back towards Laurie's apartment on foot, bracing against each other. The streetlights on Guerrero fell golden and soft, and she hummed appreciatively.

"I want to go to Amsterdam," she said.

"Don't worry, we're going to legalize weed here soon."

"That's not why. I want to see Van Gogh and Vermeer."

"Only you would blather about German artists when you're drunk."

"Dutch," Laurie said. "I want to see the Dresden letter reader. It's a study in yearning. The artist wants to know what's on the woman's mind, but she's reading a letter, completely unaware of him. The painting is so mathematically precise, but its soul... its soul is unknowable..."

"Wow," Ariel said, "you don't even need weed."

"How do you know when love is real?" she asked. "Never mind me. How are you so sure of Zahida? How is she so sure of you that she doesn't mind that you're going to crash on my couch tonight?"

Ariel's face took on a fond look. "She loved me before I transitioned. She saw me—the real me—even before I saw myself. We're forever."

"Mal sees me as an affogato."

At Ariel's perplexed look, she started giggling again, and they got home. Laurie brought out pillows and a duvet for her. Deep down, she couldn't help but think maybe Mal had always seen her too. She just couldn't be sure if she'd liked what she'd seen.

Let's talk tomorrow, she texted Mal.

One way or another, she had to know.

Forever.

That was what she wanted. She started laughing again, this time at herself. How, in this ephemeral city that went through earthquakes and fires and dotcom busts, where every young woman had had to learn the plural of apocalypse, did she dare fathom the word?

Then again, this was also the land of role-playing games and virtual reality, of artificial intelligence and spiritual transcendence, where people spoke just as seriously of going to Mars as they did of achieving godhood. Of course she'd grown used to desiring the impossible, to living only fictions.

• • •

Someone was ringing the doorbell. Had she ordered something from Amazon and forgotten about it? Laurie stepped out of her room, startling when she saw Ariel before she remembered she'd spent the night. Ariel blinked awake from the couch.

Laurie answered the door. "Who is it?"

"It's me."

What was Mal doing here? Ariel glared at her and Laurie threw up her hands.

"Are you going to let me up or are you coming down?"

Ariel folded her arms.

"Uh, just a minute." Laurie replaced the receiver and ran to her room. What was the last text she'd sent?

Let's talk tomorrow.
Foreign Cinema at 11?
Yes.

She didn't remember sending that last text. And now it was already ten-forty, and she wasn't dressed. She couldn't make Mal wait on the street so she let her up. Mal bounded up the stairs, coming to a sudden stop when she saw Ariel in the hallway.

"Oh, I didn't realize you had a new roommate."

"I'm not her roommate. I just stayed over. I'm Ariel."

"Ah, the activist," Mal said. "Laurie's told me a lot about you."

"I'll get dressed," Laurie said, heading into her room. "Sorry, we had a late night."

"No worries," she heard through the door.

"She's told me a lot about you too," Ariel said, her tone dripping with insinuation. What was she doing, starting a fight?

"Cool," Mal said, missing the bait entirely.

"Laurie, I think I'll head out," Ariel called loudly. "Take care, all right? It does no one any good to be in a state of prolonged *thirst*, however warranted."

Laurie glared at the closed door. Her friends. Always looking for ways to embarrass her.

"Yeah, it's important to hydrate after a late night out," Mal said. "Can I get you some water before you go?"

"Wow," Ariel said, and headed out without a reply. The door closed softly behind her. Laurie glanced at the mirror. Was her face beet-red again? Yes, it was. Did she have green concealer to hide it a little? Yes, in both bulk and travel size. When embarrassment met eczema, it became a necessity.

They got to Foreign Cinema around 11:30, when it would ordinarily be impossible to get a table without an hour's wait, but of course the staff saw Mal and pulled them aside. They ordered, then they both looked awkwardly at their laps, like children at detention.

Was this a date? Could you go on a first date after living together for years?

"We don't have to talk if you don't want to," Mal said. "When I suggested we meet here, I wasn't thinking about how we'd be out in public. I was going to suggest a change of venue, but then you said yes and I didn't want to chance you changing your mind."

She was rambling nervously, her leg twitching a hundred beats per minute below the table. Laurie wanted to reach out to touch her hand on the table, to calm her down, but she didn't dare. In the weeks they'd been apart she'd forgotten exactly how magnetic Mal was, practically sparking with coiled up electricity that made it impossible to look away from her fingertips.

"Can you just..." Mal took a breath and slowed down. "Would you mind telling me why the Ithaca house made you so angry? I thought you liked it. It's been driving me crazy. Things changed after that, but I don't know why."

"It was a beautiful house," Laurie acknowledged. "But it also made me realize how different our positions are. If I get kicked out of my apartment, I'd be priced out of San Francisco. You can buy a house for cash and pay a studio rent here besides."

"But the money has never bothered you before."

"It has, but I never said anything." When Mal looked hurt, she added hastily, "Not all the time. I *love* that I don't have to ask, that you'll pay the bills when we go out, that you spoiled me all the time with wine and ice-cream and spa appointments."

"So what was so different about the house?"

Their waiter served them their brunch. He seemed to recognize that all was not well, because he didn't make the usual small talk about the omelette that advertised itself as robust, or the new wave of oat milk that was quickly replacing soy.

"I guess it brought home that *this*—" Laurie gestured between them expansively, including the impressive array of fancy food—"was temporary. One day, you'd leave. If I asked you to go, it would at least be on my terms. I wouldn't be caught off guard."

"I still don't understand. What do you mean, I'd leave?"

"To your house in Ithaca."

Mal blinked in confusion. "Laurie, I bought the house for *us*. So we'd have a summer getaway, and you could visit your mother more often."

The matchstick fry in her hand fell to the floor.

"I asked you what you thought and you said you could paint for hours in the light from the windows. I wanted to give you something special. What did you think I was doing? Rubbing your face in a house you couldn't share? You think I'd do that?"

Mal was staring at her, eyes glistening, desperately wide. Needing her to answer, but she couldn't. She felt sick, at once second-guessing every conversation they'd ever had and trying to think of how to respond now.

She'd taken too long to answer. As usual. Mal got up and walked to the bathroom while Laurie stayed and stared at her meal, unable to take a bite.

Mal came back eventually, a fake smile stretched over her

face that never reached her eyes. They picked at their meals, neither of them willing to speak any more.

chapter sixteen

just when Laurie thought the year might end without any further drama, two things happened in quick succession. The Darling bought the Unicorn, making Vic her coworker once more. And the celebratory, unified holiday party would be held on a luxury yacht. Once aboard, they wouldn't be able to leave until the yacht docked. There were few things she wanted less than to be stuck on a boat among a thousand drunk techies, but as an admin she had no choice but to go.

One of the other admins came by to give her Mal's wristband for the party.

"She never came by to pick it up, and I remembered you live together."

They didn't anymore, but the HR systems hadn't been updated. Laurie took the wristband. Beyond the stabbing pain was guilty thrill. An excuse to visit Mal. She stopped by after work on a Wednesday, and Tara let her in.

"She's in her room, packing."

"Packing?"

"Says she needs a road trip." Tara gave her a pointed look. "What did you do?"

"I sabotaged us."

Tara nodded sagely. "Yeah, that tracks. You have that look about you."

"What look?"

"The look of someone who'd panic and drown in three feet of water because someone once told you that you couldn't swim."

"Hey!"

"What's going on?" Mal asked, opening the door. She stared at Laurie and pursed her lips. "What brought you here?"

"You never picked up your wristband," Laurie said, fishing in her purse. "Here."

Mal took it from her, carefully not touching her fingers. Twirled it around her thumb. "You didn't have to bring it by. I wasn't planning on going."

"I wish you would. I *have* to go, and I'm not looking forward to running into Vic."

"Why? You didn't betray him by taking up a new job. *He* laid *you* off."

Laurie glanced at Tara in reflex, but the sting of shame was gone. After everything they'd all been through together, it seemed like such a small thing.

"Besides," Mal said, "I was thinking of going south, all the way to Mexico. Do you know I've never been?"

"Neither have I," Laurie said. Tara inched away subtly, leaving them the illusion of privacy, although in the small apartment she'd be able to hear them.

"You could come," Mal said softly. Uncertainly.

"Do you want me to?"

"I don't want you to feel obligated to do anything you don't want to."

An impasse. God, Laurie wanted to go with her. Screw the

party, she could already feel the heat of the Mexican sun. She ached at once for the safe predictability of her clean, bright studio and for this other life, the passenger seat of a rented car and the slakeless thirst for adventure.

"I have to go to the party. My team is counting on me. You know one of them is going to get stuck and I'll have to delay the departure, and another one's going to be throwing up off the side of the boat."

"Babies," Mal scoffed. "Were we ever that stupid?"

Back at the Unicorn? *Yes.*

"We were worse, and you know it. We didn't even have an HR department."

Mal wandered into her bedroom. "Speaking of HR, it hit me the other day, that at my seniority, dating someone at work would probably be an abuse of power."

Laurie followed her, knowing she was skirting around something important.

"Tell me something honestly, and I swear Laurie if you lie to me about this I'll never speak to you again."

"I promise," she whispered.

"Did you ever agree to something just because I wanted it?"

"No!" She recoiled at the suggestion.

"So, that night—"

"Is that what's been eating at you? No, I was there, I wanted it, you didn't force me. God, Mal, how could you think that?"

"Well, what else was I supposed to think? You looked *green* the next day, you practically ran away and didn't speak to me for weeks, and I know I can be… *forceful*."

"You didn't do anything I didn't want. You never have."

Mal whirled around to face her. "Then *why* are you so mad at me? Just *tell me what I did!* Whatever it was, whatever made you think I was using you, I swear I'll stop it."

Tears stung her eyes. It *hurt* to see Mal in such pain, pain she'd caused with her own doubts and fears. "I'm not mad, okay? I'm *scared*, and—" Mal flinched away, and Laurie quickly corrected, "Not scared of you. Never scared of you."

"Maybe you should be," Mal said. "You have no idea how much I want...."

"Tell me."

"No." She knelt to stuff clothes into her backpack.

Laurie hadn't thought it was possible to fold underwear angrily, but Mal's disregard for the impossible was always legendary.

"I wanted to feel safe," Laurie said finally. "But you'd always said, if you can't leave, it's not love."

Mal's shoulders tightened, but she said nothing.

"You forget I'm older than you," Laurie went on. "I can't still be doing this when I'm fifty, hustling crazy, stressful work hours just to keep my health insurance, not being able to save for retirement because I have to pay the rent. Mal, you let me taste a life I never thought I'd get to have. I didn't want to get greedy and ask for more."

"But you wanted more?" she asked without looking up.

"I wanted more." Admitting it hurt, made the disappointment real.

"You could still have it," Mal said. "New York recognizes gay marriage, and we could write a prenup if it would make you feel safe."

Laurie blinked, unable to process the words. When she did, she reached for the table to hold herself up. Then she started laughing. Her breath came in heaves, as if her lungs were wet with tears.

"Mal, only you would propose *angrily*. You're so mad at me you can't even meet my eyes, and you think we should get married?"

"Isn't that what you said you wanted?" Mal asked, looking mulish.

"Not if it's not what you want, and—" Laurie put out a hand to stop her protest—"I *know* it's not what you want. Not really, or you'd have asked a long time ago. You aren't exactly a beacon of impulse control."

Mal looked so lost, so forlorn, she wanted to take her in her arms, except she had the feeling it wouldn't go over well. Even if she hadn't really meant to propose, Laurie could tell she'd hurt her pride by refusing. She asked Mal one more time to consider coming to the party, and then left. Tara had clearly been eavesdropping, but didn't say anything to her on the way out.

It was only when she got home that it hit her. Her first proposal. She sat down on the sofa, stunned. She had said *no*.

• • •

On the night of the party, Laurie managed to shepherd her team up the gangway without any sprained ankles. A woman from Sales in pencil heels wasn't as lucky. Laurie kept to herself, wandering around the yacht so nobody would see her standing around and decide to make conversation. She felt split and superimposed upon her own past. She remembered vividly how awed she'd been when she first came to the Darling's party with Sophia, but now that she worked here, now that she'd organized reward trips to Belize with swim-up bars and negotiated for private security for their executives at Ben Gurion, the wall of donuts made her stomach hurt, the photo booth set up at the bow to allow couples a chance to pose as if they were on the Titanic seemed childish, and the sumo suits with which people could wrestle each other to the ground were just plain ridiculous.

Maybe she'd grown too old for such things. As her coworkers bench-pressed each other laughingly to show off, she simply shook her head and moved on, into one of the other cabins. Of course, with her luck, she ended up directly in Vic's sights. He was already drunk.

"LAURIE!" he bellowed, and everyone's heads turned to her. She kept a polite smile on her face.

"Laurie, you have no idea how things fell apart after you left."

After you fired me. Asshole.

He turned to his gaggle of tall male friends and fake-whispered, "Laurie's a witch. She runs the place like magic, but when she left I could swear we were cursed. Nobody knew where anything was. I missed a dozen meetings. Our valuation fell."

She looked for a way out. Short of turning and running, there seemed to be no options. When she turned, her exit had been closed off.

"And now we're all here," Vic said dramatically. "All those dreams of making it on our own, running our own startups and retiring to our private islands, and here we are, corporate tools with golden handcuffs."

She smiled and started inching away, when one of the other men frowned. "Do I know you?"

"Laurie Lamont. I'm an admin."

"Yes, of course, Laurie. You were here years ago, weren't you?"

"I have no idea what you mean."

"I have an eidetic memory. I never forget a face. You fell in the water."

Laurie gulped, promptly choking and coughing in graceless surprise.

"You were here with Sophia Melnyk. Her artist girlfriend."

This couldn't be the same guy, not after all these years. She couldn't be *this* unlucky.

"What are you talking about?" Vic asked.

She stepped back, but the men had closed the circle to listen.

"Are the two of you still dating?"

"Laurie's not a lesbian," Vic said, laughing. "You aren't, are you?"

She needed to get out of here.

"No more than I am," said a familiar, beloved voice. A voice that sounded like a blade.

"Mal! You're here too! We just need to find Nick and get the old gang back together."

"Sure," Mal said. "We'll go find him."

She placed a hand on Laurie's wrist, gently guiding. Laurie followed her out of the room and into a quieter cabin, a smoking lounge with a bridge and pool table and some leather chairs.

"You okay?"

"I wish it didn't bother me so much," Laurie said. "I mean, these days everyone's trying to fly their rainbow flag from a higher hill."

"Doesn't mean coming out got any easier, especially when it's not your own choice."

Mal leaned against the pool table, completely unaware of the effect she had. All these years of living with her, Laurie had learned to ignore it, but after a few weeks apart...

"Did you ever come out? I guess I've never asked."

"I was never really in," Mal said. "My first kiss was with a girl, at a school dance. As you said before, I'm not really one for impulse control."

"What happened?" Laurie asked, overwhelmed by the thought of people jeering at a littler Mal, one who hadn't yet built up her defenses.

"She freaked out and ran away, and I stuck to kissing boys instead."

"But at least no one bullied you, or called you names?"

She shrugged. "Maybe they did. I wasn't listening."

"How do you do it? Shut out all those voices?" Laurie traced the smooth wooden edge of the pool table, her fingers inches from Mal's. "How is it you always know what you want?"

"I thought that was what it meant to be American," Mal said with a sardonic smile. "To feel the insatiability of desire. I don't know, a lot of things turn me on, I never thought to label it. Men, women, horses, Luca Guadagnino films… It's like my whole body is alive, my toes tingle, my heart pounds, and colors seem more saturated than they do on Smallville."

Why had Laurie ever thought she was a contained explosion? Mal wasn't contained at all, nothing *could* contain her.

"And me? If you felt… why did you never—?"

"*If I felt*," she scoffed, and muttered something inaudible. "You're the *reason* I felt all these things. After my dad died, I was so numb, for so long, and you… you notice everything, you feel everything, you're like a copper wire stripped of insulation. When you fall asleep in the car I want to splash you with ice water. When you're watching TV in that ridiculous Snuggie I want to fold you in half and squash you so you pay attention to me instead. I want to take you everywhere just to see that wonder in your eyes, to listen to you moan when you eat tiramisu, to watch you pet stray cats as if there couldn't be anything more to life than that."

Laurie started laughing. She hadn't thought anything could beat the proposal, but this had to be the strangest declaration of love anyone had ever made.

"And that's the best of all. You laugh like rain on a pond, the most intensely musical sound."

"You love me," she said, struck with wonder.

"Of course. Idiot."

Mal was still hovering about six feet away, waiting for her.

Oh.

She'd *always* been waiting for Laurie to make the first move.

Suddenly it was as if she was truly seeing Mal for the first time, this woman who shone so bright that so many had scattered under her relentless attention or her merciless tongue. She'd held herself back from Laurie because she was afraid of scaring her away.

Because Mal wanted her that much *more* than the things she actually went after.

As if Laurie would ever tire of her. As if she couldn't soak up every bit of what Mal had to give and still want more.

She walked up to the cabin door and locked it. Rested her head against the cool metal for a moment.

She took a deep breath, then turned around to face Mal. "Get on the table."

Mal's eyes widened comically, but she scrambled to obey so quickly that she sat on the pool table instead of the one Laurie had meant. Well, no matter.

Slowly, silently, Laurie slid the cocktail dress off Mal's shoulders. Mal waited patiently while she undid the clasp of her bra, and lay back on the pool table and raised her hips so Laurie could strip her fully.

"All your coworkers are right outside that door," Laurie whispered. "If you make too much noise, they'll hear you."

Mal shivered, and goose bumps appeared on her long, dark arms. Laurie smoothed them down but didn't do anything else, leaving her quivering on the pool table. Mal pulled her lips into her mouth and dragged her teeth against them.

I wasn't wrong.

"All those men out there are terrified of you. You say the word and they jump." Laurie met her gaze. "And you hate it."

Mal nodded mutely, her face slackening in utter gratitude at yielding control.

Laurie touched her slowly, straining her patience with tenderness, parting her legs and taking her time just looking, smelling, leaving small, feather-light kisses down the insides of her thighs. She had yet to kiss her mouth, and at times Mal lifted herself up on her elbows trying to reach her face, but eventually lay back and let Laurie set the pace.

She lapped at those secret places that tasted of the sea. Mal's legs clenched with the effort not to crush her head between them.

Eventually, Mal relaxed, and it was the most beautiful thing Laurie had ever seen. Mal leaned back, pillowing her head in her arms. For a moment she looked at Laurie with all the challenge and invitation of *La Maja Desnuda*, then her eyes closed and her head rolled to one side. She whined softly as Laurie entered her with three fingers, then gasped as her thumb rolled gently over her clit. The pool table was ruined—it would forever smell of her. Laurie couldn't help smiling at the thought of all the men who'd come here after, who would never know.

When Mal crunched upward at her climax, *then* Laurie kissed her.

She dove into her mouth when Mal thrust forward involuntarily, fed on her moan before it could gain voice. She held the back of Mal's neck in her free hand to keep her in place, and used it to lower her back down afterwards. But she kept her fingers where they were until Mal's legs and arms fell slack, and when she finally pulled them out, she tasted Mal and then ran her fingers over those reddened lips until Mal cleaned them off obediently.

A lurch let Laurie know they were docking. Mal, of course, had never met a moment she couldn't ruin, so she popped right up and said, "We should hurry. It's your turn."

"No," she said, stepping away and tossing Mal her clothes for good measure. "It's not something I tell you very often, but you're not turning this into a tit for tat or coming anywhere near my bits until you learn to slow down. We do this *my* way."

She'd have to help her over time to still her restless mind and limbs, to stop *trying* so damn hard all the time. She could hold out until then; Mal would love the challenge.

Nobody was sober enough to notice that they smelled of sex as they disembarked the yacht. Since Tara would be at Mal's they took an Uber back to Laurie's place. They didn't speak, but their hands met as soon as they got in the back. Mal had a wild look in her eyes. Laurie laughed, and it was a joyful reverberation that started at the base of her spine, gathering strength until it cascaded out of her mouth. The chill of the December air had filled her with a sense of urgency, and desire now pulled at her like an undertow.

They were tearing off each others' clothes before the door fully shut. Mal picked up her legs and pulled them around her waist, carried Laurie up the stairs without so much as breaking the kiss for air.

"What do you want?" Mal begged. "Please, just tell me what you want."

"You," Laurie said. "Always."

"Always," she said, nodding solemnly, as if making a vow.

chapter seventeen

In San Francisco, the light of day never fell harshly, but mornings were cold and rude all the same. Laurie was out of bed before Mal, who had never seen the inside edge of nine o' clock. It was a Saturday, and already noon on the East coast, so she called her mother before she could call to complain about Laurie's daughterly insufficiencies.

"Do you think you'll visit soon?"

"In the summer," Laurie promised.

And if she and Mal were still together then, maybe she'd even stay a while. In that house. That Mal had bought for them.

Laurie went into the studio and started to paint, since understanding what had happened last night, or the fact that an actual house on the east coast was apparently waiting for her, wasn't a real possibility.

Digital art never felt quite real. She couldn't feel close to a painting she hadn't struggled with. The tight stretch of dried paint on skin, the smell of it, the complexity and uncertainty of hue and the ache in her wrist—the markers of her love.

It occurred to her that putting up a painting on the wall was rather like getting married, as if by turning her love from a verb into a noun, a possession, she had checked something off a list.

My painting. My wife.

How strange the possessive sounded! Loud and belligerent, not like her at all.

"Good morning," Mal said. She was dressed, but wrapped up in a blanket. The heating in this house really was awful. "It's nearly ten-thirty. Shall we get brunch?"

Laurie nodded and started putting away her brushes. "Do you need to call Tara?"

"Already did." Mal rolled her eyes. "She sent me a stream of sailboat emojis and said she'd go down with the ship."

Laurie noticed she wasn't wearing the cocktail dress from last night. "Did you have a change of clothes here?"

Mal hesitated. "Actually, I had several in my backpack. I really was going to Mexico. I just figured I'd stop by the party first."

"Oh."

As they headed downstairs, Laurie started feeling uneasy. This could become a pattern. Mal wanting to go somewhere, Laurie inadvertently tying her down. Pinning her to the wall like a painting. Art and people both—how simple to mistake having them for loving them.

Mal's phone rang.

"It's Aditi."

She stepped away to speak to her sister, while Laurie stared at her profile in confusion. She loved Mal. She was as sure of that as she was that she didn't want to give up her studio so Mal could move back in. She couldn't tell if that reluctance was self-sabotage.

"I'll call you back," Mal said, and turned to Laurie, looking worried. "Aditi convinced my mother to come up to the city today. They want to get brunch with Tara before she goes back to school."

"We can catch up later."

"We both go, or neither of us goes."

"It's a family thing."

"Tara made you family when she called you that day."

When they got to brunch, Tara was scowling. Her face cleared when she saw them. Even Aditi seemed unsurprised to see Laurie, although Aditi's mother only nodded stiffly.

"I told them you two usually get brunch together," Tara said carefully.

Oh, right. They'd have arrived to see Mal wasn't home.

"I don't see why you need to stay in San Francisco if you're going to be on your own," Mal's mother said to Tara. "You might as well be at home, where we can cook for you, do your laundry."

"A meal isn't free when it comes with long faces and lectures," Tara said.

"Tara!" Aditi said.

"What? It's true."

"We just want what's best for you," said Tara's grandmother.

"Do you?" Mal asked suddenly. There was no anger or accusation in her gaze, just open curiosity. "What do you think that is?"

Her mother spluttered, as if the question was ridiculous and the answer obvious.

"No, seriously," Mal said softly, "I think we all want only the best for each other. We just disagree about what that means."

"And what do you know about raising a child? Or about what it takes to get three fatherless kids settled?"

Laurie flinched. Mal didn't react. Instead her brows furrowed, and she took on that calm, managerial voice that Laurie had only ever heard her use at work. "Getting us settled. What does that mean to you?"

"The same thing it means to anyone with a lick of sense. A good job. A house. A marriage and kids."

Aditi added, "That's later, though. Right now, it means good grades and good friends, not partying and coming home to a street covered in shit and heroin needles."

"And if she had these things," Mal asked, "a house, a job, a marriage and kids, do you think she'd be happy?"

"She'd be *safe*," Aditi said, casting a worried glance at Tara, who was watching the exchange with held breath.

"Safe from what?" Mal asked, with that calm stillness in her voice, but a glance below the table showed Laurie her restless, bouncing knee.

"What kind of a question is that?" Aditi asked. She looked at her nearly empty brunch plate as if it might offer her a reprieve.

"You've both said the same things to me a hundred times. My grades were never high enough, my job—"

"That's because you never *tried*!" Mal's mother said. "You could have gone to college at fourteen if you'd bothered."

"But *why*?"

"What do you mean, why? How can you have such gifts and *squander* them? The rest of the world would kill for a fraction of your talent, and you… you just…"

Mal took a deep breath, and exhaled. "This was never about me, was it? Mom, a 4.0 GPA can't prevent cancer. There's nothing we could have done to be safer."

"That's not what we're saying," Aditi said. "You're twisting our words."

"Then explain," Mal said. Her fingers clenched inside her linen napkin.

Laurie had been silent, unable to speak past the flood of emotion in her chest. Mal's profile, tense but focused, was so different from the image burned into her memory, of her standing on a deck in Tahoe with her wet hair rolling down her shoulders, whooping with joy into the mountains at finally being free.

She slid her hand over Mal's leg, quieting the restless twitch there. It wasn't much, but Mal threw her a grateful look and placed her own hand on top of Laurie's.

"Maybe we should talk about this later," Aditi said. "We're making Laurie uncomfortable."

Silence fell over the table. Somehow, in an instant, it was her move. She'd only been listening. But if she said nothing, if she conceded to her discomfort and retreated to the bathroom for a bit, this would only drag on forever, each of them insistent and unyielding in their own way, never actually listening to each other.

And this was *her* family now too.

"I don't mind," she said. "There may not be a later time for everyone to talk more. In January, Tara's going back to college and before that, Mal and I are going to Mexico."

Mal shot her a look of surprise, but a smile broke out over her face.

"When?" Aditi asked.

"Mexico?" her mother asked. "What for?"

"For a holiday," Mal said. "Right now, in fact."

"A *holiday*?" her mother shrieked. "The family's in crisis, Tara's spiraling out of control, and you're going to leave and go to Mexico?"

Under the table, Laurie's fingers threaded through Mal's and held tight. Mal squeezed back.

"She's not abandoning me," Tara said. "She's giving me the room to show I've learned my lesson."

Laurie had never heard her tone sound quite like that—respectful and reserved. She reminded herself to tell Mal, later, how good she was with Tara. That she shouldn't listen to all those who said she was screwing this up. Not that she would, but maybe it was time Laurie pulled her weight and tried anyway. She ran her thumb soothingly along the back of Mal's hand.

"This is nothing against you, personally, Laurie," Aditi said hastily. "We're just trying to understand."

"What's to understand?" her mother asked, sneering at Mal. "You're just like your father. When things get hard, you run. You don't care who you hurt or leave behind."

That, finally, made Mal flinch. Her fingers started to pull away.

"That's not true," Laurie said, tightening her grip.

Everyone's eyes turned to her, but she couldn't stay silent anymore. "She doesn't have to deal with any of this, but she does. I've never met anyone as generous, as forgiving, as patient. So many people have tried to hurt her or cut her down, but she ignores them and doesn't hold a grudge. And any time anyone needs her, she drops *everything* to be with them."

She wanted to tell them that even last night, Mal had been so hurt by the distance Laurie had put between them, but she'd put aside all her grievances and come to the party just for her. And this morning, Laurie could tell she wasn't settled—*they* weren't settled—but she'd postponed Mexico and come to this painful brunch so Tara wouldn't be alone.

"You all say you care," Tara added in a small voice, "but Mal's the one researching how to seal or expunge my record. Dad's not even answering my calls."

"He's just hurt," Aditi said.

"And his feelings matter more than Tara's future?" Mal asked. Again, she'd somehow managed to ask without accusation, as if it were a genuine question upon which she wished instruction.

"No, I just meant if you came home, if he saw that you needed him—"

"—but I don't though," Tara said.

"Tara, you can't say that," Aditi said. "You always need family."

"Yes, and my family came through for me when I needed them," Tara said, looking at Mal and Laurie with open, unreserved affection.

"Laurie's been a good friend," Mal's mother conceded, sounding as if it took her a lot to do so, "but family is something else. It's—"

"—Unconditional?" Tara asked, chin jutting out in challenge.

"Supportive," Mal added, squeezing her hand.

"Forgiving," Aditi said, and Laurie stared at her in surprise.

"Unwavering," Laurie whispered, so only Mal could hear her.

Mal's mother looked around the table, then more closely at the two of them. Her eyes widened and she leaned back with a startled cry. "Wait a minute. You're not... you two aren't..."

Laurie turned to Mal, and answered the question in her eyes with a smile.

Mal lifted their joined hands from underneath the table and placed them in full view of everyone.

"We are," she said, simply.

Tara squealed so loudly she sent a knife to the floor, and then started shouting all sorts of things—*I knew it, it's about time, you two are idiots*—but Laurie wasn't listening.

Until Mal had said it, Laurie hadn't realized how much she'd needed to hear it, and how perfect the answer was.

We are.

She turned to Mal's mother, hoping she wouldn't see too much condemnation there. Strangely, there wasn't any. There was terror though, and a lot of it. The older woman cast her eyes around the restaurant hurriedly, as if to see who might be watching, listening, whispering.

It was like looking in a funhouse mirror, if she'd let fear and shame become her inheritance, if she hadn't walked into the light.

"It's all right," she told her. "We're safe."

"We should celebrate," Tara said. "Maybe get a bottle of champagne?" All heads turned to her. "For you, not for *me*!"

"We can get *smoothies*," Aditi said sternly.

"Smoothies are fine too." Tara turned to them. "So, are you going to get married?"

"Tara!" Aditi said.

"Well, I asked and she said no, and it's not legal in California anyway," Mal said.

"It will be," Tara said firmly. "And she only said no because your proposal was terrible."

"Let's maybe leave them to tell us their plans when they're ready?" Aditi asked, her throat straining with embarrassment.

"But they have to have a big wedding," Mal's mother said suddenly. When they all stared at her, she shrugged. "What's done is done. I don't care who you marry, but you have to get married."

Mal groaned. "Baby steps."

"You really are like him, you know," her mother said. "Once you get an idea in your mind, nothing can stop you."

"Speaking of which," Laurie said, seeing the opening, "Don't we have somewhere to be?"

Mal shot her a grateful look. They said goodbye to the others, and made sure Tara had her spare keys and enough cash for the cleaners. Laurie stepped aside and let her boss know she'd be out through the end of the year, although he wasn't planning to come to work after Tuesday either anyway.

"You did this, you know," Aditi said, coming up to her.

"Did what?"

"Oh, sorry, I meant that in a good way. Mal's always lived in her own world. When she was little, we couldn't even get her to talk to guests or stop reading at dinner. Mom always thought it meant she didn't care about people. But you've anchored her."

Laurie frowned. "I hope not."

"It's a good thing," Aditi said. "She wants both to be in the world but free of it. To understand people but not be beholden to them. To soar away and explore, but always be able to come back home on her own terms." She surprised Laurie with a warm, strong hug. "You give her that."

Mal and Laurie walked to the Enterprise center and got in the little Chevy she'd booked, since a Zipcar couldn't be taken across the border.

"Are you sure about this?" Mal asked. "I could also just drop you off at home if you've changed your mind. And don't you need to pack?"

"My bag's ready. We could also just buy anything we need along the way."

"We could."

Mal grinned and put the car into gear. Within an hour they were on the freeway. Soon, they left behind the endless glass and silicon towers for the soft, fuzzy hills near San Jose.

"This trip," Mal said hesitantly, "I decided I had to go because of a dream I had."

"Okay." She didn't need to justify herself, but Laurie was happy to listen.

"Everyone's souls were candles, and they were guarding their candles in shrines and going to work without them. If you wanted to see someone's soul, they'd put you through a series of trials. Except my soul wasn't a candle."

"Oh?"

"It was a laser. People were attracted to it from a distance, but if they got close they either ran away scared or got burned to cinders."

"Mal," she sighed.

"You're the only one who operates on my frequency. With everyone else, I have to turn it down."

Laurie slid her hand into Mal's and let her tears roll down uninterrupted. There was no reason to hide them. There never would be again.

They passed Monterey, where Laurie had organized strategy meetings through which engineers and venture capitalists would somehow stay focused despite the whales and dolphins in the background, and the bay at Moss Landing where she'd run a dozen team-building kayaking trips. It felt good to leave it all behind, to cut off all the umbilical cords and make space for something new.

Something *now*.

She felt it then, the same hum of the road that had sent both of them and so many others to this golden coast in search of magic and insight, the certainty that this was all there was to home in America, to yield to the gut-lurch of the accelerator and lean forward into the next crazy venture beneath this illimitable sky.

acknowledgements

This book almost didn't happen. After years of rejections of the "Your writing is fantastic but I don't know if there's a market for this" variety, I put this novel aside. One day, a friend sent me some of his own writing. As an introvert who used to write with a blanket over my head so nobody would see, I understood the courage it took to share. In return, I shared the manuscript of *Her Golden Coast*. His incredible response made me realize I had, like so many in tech, conflated worth with profitability. I had propped up gatekeepers to tell me *No*, compromising my desires before reaching for them.

Thank you, Jay, for resuscitating this story.

Her Golden Coast is a labor of love, from cover to cover. If you read through to the end, my editor Caroline Manring is to thank for it. She uncovered my true meaning from all the cruft and cowardice under which it was buried—her poet's sharp eyes and ears allowed the story to match my intention that it should read "as if in a single breath," in the stream of consciousness prose style of the Beat Generation.

My thanks to Mark Spencer and Terri Valentine for their encouraging and constructive feedback on various drafts, to Osman Haneef, Kia Abdullah and Caroline Manring for reading this book and sharing their thoughts, and to Vanessa Mendozzi for designing the book and its cover. I can't possibly name all the incredible women in tech I've had the luck to work with over the years, but there is a little of each of you in here.

Two people deserve special mention: my admin, Regina Sanchez, who is just as incredible and underestimated as Laurie is, without whom I would be crying on my couch, too stressed out to remember my own name. And, of course, Sami jo, my muse, who tolerates holiday trips where I regale her with plot lines and half-baked drafts, and who challenges me every day to go after my dreams.

And, of course, there would be no book without you, dear readers! Thank you for coming along for the ride. I hope you'll feed the algorithms of the capitalist machine and leave reviews for me on Amazon and Goodreads, but more importantly, if you can think of someone in your life who might enjoy this book, please share it with them.

Thank you!

about the author

anat Deracine writes on the themes of women's friendships and relationships, and their struggles with oppressive social structures. Her first novel, *Driving by Starlight* (Macmillan, 2018) received starred reviews from Publishers Weekly and Kirkus for its portrayal of young women growing up under the scrutiny of the religious police in Saudi Arabia.

She is currently at work on an adult fantasy series. Join her mailing list at **deracine.substack.com** to be the first to read it!